A Summer Secret

Books for Adults by Kathleen Fuller:

A Man of His Word

An Honest Love

A Summer Secret

Book One: The Mysteries of Middlefield Series

by Kathleen Fuller

A Division of Thomas Nelson Publishers

NASHVILLE   DALLAS   MEXICO CITY   RIO DE JANEIRO

Published in Nashville, Tennessee, by Tommy Nelson®. Tommy Nelson is a registered trademark of Thomas Nelson, Inc.

Thomas Nelson, Inc., titles may be purchased in bulk for educational, business, fund-raising, or sales promotional use. For information, please e-mail SpecialMarkets@ThomasNelson.com.

Library of Congress Cataloging-in-Publication Data

ISBN 978-1-4003-1593-2

Printed in the United States of America

10 11 12 13 14 RRD 5 4 3

Mfg. by RRD
Crawfordsville, Indiana
MAY 2010
PPO# 108588

To my family. *Danki.*

Acknowledgments

THANK YOU to the wonderful editors who helped me so much during the writing of this book: MacKenzie Howard, Jamie Chavez, Laura Minchew, and Natalie Hanemann. I couldn't have done it without you. A special thank-you to my daughter Zoie for helping me brainstorm and keeping me on track. I love you.

A Note from the Author

A Summer Secret is set in the village of Middlefield, Ohio, in northeast Ohio near Cleveland. Established in 1885, Middlefield is the fourth-largest Amish settlement in the world. Here Amish buggies share the gently sloping roads with "Yankee" cars and motorcycles.

Many of the Middlefield Amish, like the Lancaster County Amish, are Old Order. While both the Middlefield and Lancaster settlements are divided into districts, each with its own *Ordnung*—an unwritten set of rules members abide by—there are noticeable differences in buggy style, dress, and cultural influence. In Middlefield, non-Amish are referred to as *Yankees*, while in Lancaster they are called *Englischers*. A Lancaster Amish man might drive a gray-colored buggy, while Middlefield buggies are always black. A Middlefield woman's prayer *kapp* at first glance might look the same as a Lancaster *kapp*, yet upon deeper inspection they are of differing design. There are also varying guidelines for the use of technology. While these superficial differences are evident among all Amish settlements, they do not detract from the main tenets of the Amish faith—a desire to grow closer to God, the importance of family and community, and a plain and humble lifestyle.

With the help of some extremely generous Amish and Yankee friends, I have tried to portray the Amish in Middlefield as accurately and respectfully as possible. If there are any mistakes or misconceptions in my story, they are of my own making.

—Kathleen Fuller

Glossary of Amish Terms

ab im kopp: crazy
boppli: baby
bruders: brothers
bu: boy
buwe: boys
Daed: Dad
danki: thank you
Dietch: name of language
dochder: daughter
dumm: dumb
Fraa: Mrs.
geh: go
gut: good
guten morgen: good morning
halt: stop, halt
Herr: Mister (Mr.)
kapp: prayer covering worn by women and girls

kind: child
kinder: children
Mami: Mom, Mommy
mutter: mother
nachtesse: dinner
nee: no
nix: nothing
onkel: uncle
seltsam: strange, weird
sohn: son
ya: yes

One

June 2

IT'S NOT *fair. Nothing in my life is fair.*

Mary Beth Mullet stared at the words in her journal. She took a deep breath, inhaled the faint scent of pig on her skin, and let out a long sigh. She'd probably have to take two baths tonight. Maybe after that the stench would go away. Mary Beth had never realized how bad the pigs smelled until she had fallen into that gross mud in their pen. She wasn't even supposed to feed them this morning. That was usually her twin brother Johnny's job, but he had been helping hitch up Crackerjack to the buggy. She flipped over a couple of pages until she found a clean sheet of paper and began to draw, an activity that always settled her down. There were still a few parts of the barn that she hadn't sketched in her journal over the past several weeks.

Hearing the tweeting of a swallow, she looked up in the corner of the barn, noticing for the first time the nest tucked in the rafters. Applying pencil to paper, she quickly outlined the corner of the barn before adding the swallow and the nest. Were there eggs in the nest? She didn't know and couldn't find out since the ceiling of the barn was so high. She added three tiny eggs to her drawing anyway, carefully coloring little bitty dots on each one. She had no idea if swallows had speckled eggs, but she liked the extra detail.

When she finished her drawing, she closed her journal, placed it on the matted straw beside her, and stood up. She had started coming here when school let out in April, mostly as an escape from Johnny and her younger brothers, Caleb and Micah. Now it was the second week in June, and she hated to think this might be the last summer she spent here. After finishing eighth grade next year, she would probably be expected to get a job outside the house. But she didn't want to think about that right now. She was thirteen and still had one more year to enjoy her freedom. She planned to spend as much time here as she possibly could.

But right now she needed to get home before she was missed. As she always did before she left, she picked up her blanket, shook out the strands of straw clinging to it, then neatly folded it. Tucking her journal underneath the blanket, she checked her stash of supplies—several small boxes of juice, a few granola bars, a packet of graham crackers, and one apple in a plastic baggie. Glancing around, she remembered what her father had said about the barn: he had told her not to go near it. "That old thing is on its last legs," her *daed* had said. If her parents knew she was here, she would be in big trouble.

Still, Mary Beth didn't think it was so bad. Sure, the wood was black with rot, and the entire barn leaned to the left. Huge gaps were in the wall where slats used to be, and the whole place smelled kind of musty, especially on really hot days. But there were enough holes in the walls to let in plenty of light, yet keep her dry when it rained. Anyone could see this barn had character—and it was *her* place. The one spot where she could be alone to read, to draw, to dream. Here she didn't have to worry about her brothers bugging her or her parents asking her to do something she didn't want to do. She snuck away to her special place whenever she had a chance.

The sunbeams had shifted from the east side of the barn to the west, and she knew her mother would be calling for her to help with supper. After making one last check of her supplies, she started to head for home when she noticed something glinting on the dirt floor. She knelt down and brushed away the dirt. A button. She picked it up. It was small and round, had four holes, and was made of a brass-colored metal.

Mary Beth frowned. The Amish didn't wear buttons. They used straight pins to fasten their clothes. Buttons were considered too fancy. *How did this get here?*

Mary Beth tucked the button in her fist and left the barn running. She ran across the field of thick grass that reached almost to her waist. The blades tickled her legs and bare feet as she made her way through them. The long strings of her black prayer *kapp* trailing behind her, she made it home in record time. But as she got close to the door, she saw something move out of the corner of her eye. Turning, she saw a black-and-white dog sitting near the back step, looking at her with big brown eyes.

"Where did you come from?" The dog was cute, but she didn't approach it. Stray dogs could be dangerous, and she had never seen this one before. The animal looked well kept, though. Its fur shone in the early evening sunlight, and it had a stout body, as if it hadn't missed a meal.

The dog didn't move, just wagged its tail and continued to look at her. Mary Beth grinned and then went inside. Soon enough the dog would get bored and move on, probably back to its owner.

"There you are, Mary Beth," *Mami* said as Mary Beth burst into the kitchen. Her mother shut off the sink and shook the water from her hands. "I was just about to call you. The potatoes need peeling."

"What's for *nachtesse*?" she asked, walking toward the stove.

"Shepherd's pie."

Mary Beth made a face. She hated shepherd's pie. Plus this was the third time in two weeks they'd had it. Why couldn't they have pizza every once in a while? Or McDonald's? But she didn't dare ask her mother for take-out food. More than once she had overheard her parents talking about money, their voices worried and hushed. Mary Beth didn't understand, because both her parents worked. Her mother made jackets and coats and sold them to a woman who owned a small shop in Parkman. Just last week she had started on a quilt she said she hoped would bring a good price. Yet one glance at her *mami's* worn work dress, with the hole in the frayed bottom hem, told her that money was tight, despite her mother and father working hard every day.

So shepherd's pie it would be, made with potatoes, green beans, and tomato sauce canned from their garden, plus hamburger from the cow they raised last year. Since there were no pockets in her dress, Mary Beth ran upstairs and put the button under her pillow, then dashed down to the basement to get the ingredients for supper.

She emerged a few moments later to chaos.

"Caleb, *halt!*" Her mother put her hand up in front of Mary Beth's ten-year-old brother. "How many times have I told you to leave your muddy shoes by the back door? You're tracking dirt all over my kitchen floor!"

Caleb shrugged. "Sorry, *Mami.*"

But Mary Beth didn't think he looked sorry at all. She caught the smirk on his face as he passed by her on his way out of the kitchen.

"Micah, *nee!*" *Mami* rushed over to eighteen-month-old Micah, who was climbing on the kitchen cabinet nearest to the stove. She grabbed him around the waist and pulled him down. "You know you're not allowed to climb on the counters!"

"Dink." He held out his hands and repeatedly opened and closed them.

"Then you ask for a drink. Mary Beth, will you get your brother some water?"

Her hands were still filled with dinner ingredients, so she set the canned goods down, then went to the sink. After filling a cup with water from the tap, she turned to Micah.

Caleb entered the kitchen again, this time in his bare feet. "When are we gonna eat?" he asked.

"Caleb, get a broom and sweep the dirt you tracked in," *Mami* ordered.

"Why can't Mary Beth do it?"

"Because I told you to!" *Mami* leaned against the counter and wiped her shiny forehead. "Lord, give me strength," she whispered.

At that moment Johnny burst into the kitchen. "The pigs are loose!"

Mary Beth surveyed the scene in front of her—Micah shaking his sippy cup upside down and fussing, Caleb standing behind their mother and making faces, Johnny yelling one more time that the pigs had escaped their pen. The racket echoed in Mary Beth's ears.

Mami looked at Mary Beth and at the water dripping down the sides of the cabinet. "Don't just stand there—go help your brother find the pigs! I have to clean up this mess."

Mary Beth wanted to protest, but she remained silent. She knew better than to sass her mother. Although Caleb was a faster runner and had more experience chasing stray animals, she kept her mouth shut. Instead she whirled around and joined Johnny outside. After today, she never wanted to see another pig again.

She rushed outside to see one of the fat, white pigs amble over to the back of the yard, covered in stinky pig mud, its snout scraping against the ground as it snuffled for food. Any appetite she'd had for dinner disappeared as her nostrils filled with the smell.

"Mary Beth!" Johnny shouted as he appeared from the back of the barn. "I got all of them but this ornery one. Help me get him."

"What do you want me to do?"

"You get on one side, I'll get on the other. When he tries to get away, one of us will run in front of him and guide him toward the barn." He waved his arms at the hog. "C'mon, Hambone."

"Hambone? Since when did you start naming the pigs?"

"I've always named the pigs." He held his finger up to his lips. "Shh. Let him get *gut* and comfortable before we sneak up on him."

As Johnny took his position near the snorting pig, Mary Beth came up behind and walked slowly toward it. She knew from experience chasing a pig was useless. They were fat, but they were also fast. The best way was to sneak up behind them. Carefully she crept toward him. Hambone kept his head down, not suspecting a thing. But when she came within three feet of him, his head shot up and he bolted off toward the field.

"What did you do that for?" Johnny shouted, running past her.

"I did what you told me to do!"

"Well, next time, don't listen to me!" he called over his shoulder.

Mary Beth ran after Johnny and Hambone, but she couldn't keep up. Just as Johnny got close, the pig ran farther and faster, squealing and snorting into the open field toward the old abandoned barn. Johnny fell farther behind as Mary Beth came to a stop, her chest heaving. If Johnny couldn't catch up to Hambone, how would they ever get him back home?

Suddenly she heard a dog bark. The black-and-white dog she'd seen by the house appeared from the nearby grove of trees and started chasing the pig. Terrified, Hambone squealed and skidded to a stop before doing a one-eighty and running back toward his pen. Unlike Johnny and Mary Beth, the dog had no problem keeping up with Hambone, and each time the pig tried to change direction, the dog was there to herd him.

As the animals neared, Johnny whistled at the dog. "C'mon, boy! Bring Hambone over here." He waved his arm in the air, then rushed over to the back of the barn where the pig pen was.

Mary Beth watched as the dog herded Hambone right back in the pen. She saw Johnny latch the gate in place and take off his hat, leaning over the gate and gasping for breath. He glanced down at the dog sitting next to his feet, panting, its pink tongue hanging out of its mouth.

"Well, whaddya know?" Johnny sounded breathless. "A dog that herds pigs. Didn't know they could do that." He looked up at Mary Beth. "Whose dog is this, anyway?"

She shrugged, staring at the pooch. He—or she—had big

brown eyes, black ears that stood up like two triangles on top of its head, and a long white muzzle. "I don't know. It must belong to someone."

"Probably." Johnny put his hat on his head, leaned down, and stroked the dog's head. "Glad he was here."

"He?"

Johnny glanced up and gave her a pointed look. "Definitely a *he*." He patted the dog a few more times, which caused the dog's tail to thump against the ground. "Maybe if you're around after supper, *bu*, I'll sneak you a bone."

Mary Beth smirked. "We don't have any bones."

"Okay, maybe a piece of bread. He deserves a reward, *ya?*"

"*Ya*. He sure does."

As they walked to the house, the dog continued to follow them, stopping just short of the bottom step of the back deck. Instead of trying to get inside, he sat down and looked at them.

"Wish he could come inside," Johnny said, squatting in front of the dog.

"*Ya*, but you know what *Mami* said about animals in the house."

"But look at him, Mary Beth. He wants to come in."

She looked at the dog. He was still panting, but didn't look distressed. "I don't think so. He hasn't moved. Or whined. I think he's happy being right here."

"Maybe. But I'd still like him to come in. I'll ask *Daed* after supper. He likes dogs. I'll have a better chance with him than with *Mami*."

"I think he belongs to someone, Johnny."

"He doesn't have a collar." Johnny rose. "And if he did have an owner, what's he doing over here?"

"Visiting? I don't know." She opened the screen door. "We better get inside."

Johnny nodded. "Bye, *bu*," he said, then walked into the house behind her.

At last the shepherd's pie was out of the oven. Mary Beth washed up Micah and settled him in his high chair. Then she took her place and Johnny slid in beside her at the table. Everyone bowed their heads in silent prayer for a few moments, then started eating.

Daed picked up his fork with his left hand and shoved it into a pile of potatoes and meat, the movement still slightly awkward. It had been a year since his buggy had been clipped by a car on Nauvoo Road and his right hand had been crushed beneath one of the wheels. The healing process had been long, and he didn't have complete use of his hand yet. Still, he managed fine and only needed help with a few things, like hitching up Crackerjack when he was in a hurry to get to work in the morning. She'd overheard him say more than once that he was lucky to still have a job, and that he'd lost a good amount of earnings when he had to stay home and heal from the accident.

"Pass the salt," Caleb said, elbowing Mary Beth in the side. She glared at him. He arched his eyebrows in return, his chocolate brown eyes daring her to tattle on him. She wouldn't give him the satisfaction and handed him the salt without a word. Johnny slurped down his milk, which made Micah laugh. Grinning, Johnny took another drink, slurping even louder. Mary Beth frowned, annoyed.

"That's enough, Johnny." *Daed* took another forkful of food and shoved it in his mouth. "Mind your manners."

"*Ya, Daed.*"

But when Johnny stopped slurping, Micah started banging his cup against his chair, wanting him to continue. Finally their mother snatched the cup from him, putting it out of reach. Micah started to whimper.

Just a typical evening meal.

Mary Beth picked at her food. She was tired of her brothers always making a racket and causing trouble, tired of shepherd's pie, and tired of seeing the strain on her *mami's* face and the worried frown on her *daed's*. But there was nothing she could do about any of it. After supper Mary Beth helped her mother wash and dry the dishes. When she was finished, she peeked out the back door to see if the dog was still there. He wasn't. She sighed and walked back to the kitchen.

"We're going to sit outside for a little while, Mary Beth." Her mother put the last dish away in the cabinet by the sink. "It's a beautiful evening. Don't you want to join us?"

"*Nee.*" Mary Beth shook her head. She didn't really feel like being outside tonight.

"All right, but if you change your mind, come on out. It's

too beautiful an evening to be cooped up in the house." She smiled and touched Mary Beth's cheek.

While her family was outside, she ran upstairs to her room and flopped on the bed and looked up at the ceiling. She heard Caleb and Johnny shouting at each other while they played in the backyard. Suddenly remembering the button, she pulled it out from underneath her pillow. She stared at it again, her fingers sliding over the tiny holes. Maybe the button was old and had been left by the people who had owned the barn. Her *daed* said Yankees owned the property next door, but they hadn't taken care of it, and that's why the barn was in such bad shape. Perhaps the button had fallen off a Yankee's shirt a long time ago.

Mary Beth turned onto her side and closed her eyes, the barn's image forming in her mind. Only instead of a rotting shell of a building, it was a brand-new structure—freshly coated in white paint on the outside and filled with hay and animals on the inside. She could practically hear the nickering of a horse in a stall and smell the scent of clean hay. Her imagination journeyed on as she saw a man walk into the barn, wearing Yankee clothes and heading to the back corner of the barn where the cows were kept.

Her eyes flew open and she popped up from the bed and found her journal, which was hidden underneath her bed. Quickly she drew the scene, showing the faceless man carrying a tin pail to use for milking. Down by his feet was the button, which had fallen off his shirt, unnoticed. When she finished the drawing, she closed her book, satisfied that her imagination had solved the mystery of the stray button. Then again, what if someone else had been in the barn lately? She shook her head and closed her hand around the button. She didn't want to think about some stranger lurking around her special place. No, the button must have been there a long, long time. She just hadn't noticed it until today.

Two

THE NEXT day, after Mary Beth had finished her chores, she headed back to the old barn, the button fading from her memory. She ran across the field, the hot sun warming her back as she dashed through the tall grass. When she reached the barn, she stepped inside, breathing in the familiar and welcome scents of musty hay and old wood. She thought about the picture she'd drawn yesterday and smiled. Even though she had imagined a brand-new barn, she liked this old place just the same.

She walked over to her special corner and grabbed her journal. She actually had two of them, one that she kept here and another that stayed under her bed at home. She used to have only one, but she kept forgetting it in one place or the other. It was easier to have two, so she was never without a notebook to write and sketch in.

She took the journal outside and sat down behind the barn, leaning against the splintery wall, eager to find something to sketch. A couple of black and orange orioles were chasing each other near the trees. That would make a good picture.

She often thought about showing her parents her drawings, but she couldn't bring herself to do it. Like the barn, this was her secret, something she kept to herself. Sketching was fun, something she enjoyed doing to pass the time.

Flipping open her journal, she pulled the pencil out of the binding and searched for a fresh page. She thumbed through several sketches, then a few pages of her private thoughts, which she recorded from time to time. She hadn't realized the journal was almost full. Finding a clean sheet, she started to fold the previous page back when she noticed something odd. The right-hand corner was bent.

She examined it closely. Sure enough, there was a crease in the corner. She didn't dog-ear her pages and disliked it when she checked out books from the library and saw the creased corners where people had marked places in a book. She would never do something like this to her journal. But she couldn't deny that something—or someone—had.

The hair on the back of her neck started to prickle. She looked to the right and to the left, then listened carefully. All she could hear was the faint *clip-clop* of a horse and buggy going down the road in the distance, the birds singing high in the trees, and a slight breeze rustling the grass surrounding the barn. Still, she couldn't help but feel as if she were being watched.

After a few moments she took the pencil and tried to sketch the birds, but they had already left, and she couldn't do it very well from memory. Giving up, she folded over the page and tried to draw something else, trying not to think about the possibility that someone had handled her journal. But she couldn't get the thought out of her mind, and she turned back to the creased page and studied it again. Then she flipped through the book, checking for more bends, smudges, or tears in the paper. She didn't see any.

Maybe she had accidentally bent it when she put her journal down the other day when she had left in such a hurry. That had to be the answer. If someone had been looking at her journal, wouldn't there have been other clues? Hopping up from her seat, she went back inside the barn and inspected her corner. Nothing else was out of place. She shook her head. It was all very, very strange.

A couple of days later, Mary Beth was still thinking about the button and the dog-eared page in her journal. Even as she dressed for her chores, she couldn't keep the thoughts out of her mind. Had someone else really been in the barn? Had that someone gone through her things? She shuddered at the idea of anyone reading her private thoughts. But who would do that? As far as she knew, she was the only person who had been in the barn. When she'd gone inside the first time, there hadn't been a sign that anyone had been there for years.

Yet what other explanation could there be for the button? The bent page?

Realizing she was wasting time, she quickly pulled on her

light green dress and fastened the front opening at the top with a couple of straight pins. Standing in front of the small mirror on her dresser, she brushed out her long, blonde hair and put it up in a bun. Then she fastened her black prayer *kapp* in place with four black bobby pins and ran downstairs to help *Mami* with breakfast.

It was still mostly dark outside, but the sun had started to come up. Dim beams of light shone through the front room window as Mary Beth made her way to the kitchen. She could hear the hissing sound of the gas lamp as she entered the room. Being Amish, her family didn't have electricity, but they did use gas lamps and appliances. The lamp was attached to a long bar, which was hooked to a white propane tank. Her mother had set the lamp in the corner of the kitchen, flooding the room with light.

Mary Beth yawned as she looked at the battery-operated clock hanging above the doorway. It was five thirty in the morning. Her mother would start cooking soon, so Mary Beth grabbed a bowl from the countertop and went outside to fetch eggs. She crossed the short distance to the coop, which was situated behind their barn. Her feet lightly touched the soft grass as she hurried to finish the chore.

She didn't mind gathering the eggs too much. The brown hens didn't peck at her toes like the crabby old rooster did, and while chickens smelled, they weren't as stinky as the pigs. She spied the rooster strutting in front of the dingy white coops as if he were guarding the hens inside. When he saw Mary Beth approach, he crowed loudly.

"Oh, be quiet." She shooed the contrary bird away and stepped inside the chicken coop. They had ten hens that laid one egg each day in the laying boxes her *daed* had nailed against the wall. Each hen had her own little cubby filled with straw. Usually by the time Mary Beth arrived, most of the eggs had been deposited on the straw, like pearls in wooden oysters. She left the door open behind her, not only to air out the house, but to let the chickens roam the backyard. *Mami* said chickens who were allowed their freedom laid the best eggs. At night they would all go back to the chicken coop, settle into their boxes, and go to sleep. Either she or one of her brothers would close them in for the night to keep them safe from hungry foxes and coyotes roaming the woods nearby.

"*Guten morgen*," Mary Beth said to one of the hens who was still in her box. She reached underneath her warm feathers and felt around for the egg. The bird stood up, then jumped out of the coop before Mary Beth had the egg in the basket. The three remaining hens followed, and Mary Beth was able to easily collect the rest of the eggs.

As she headed back to the house, she stopped and looked at the sky. The sun looked like a half circle in the distance, part of it hidden by land. The horizon, her teacher had called it. Surrounding the sun were flat clouds tinted lavender, peach, and gold. Her ears were filled with the sounds of birds singing their wake-up songs, along with a few crows from the annoying rooster. Mary Beth felt rooted to the ground as she took in the beauty around her. She never got enough of seeing the colorful sunrises and sunsets. What she wouldn't do for her journal and pencil right now! She wished she could spend the rest of the morning sketching the lovely sky.

When Mary Beth realized she was dawdling, she hurried to the house. Inside, her brothers were already up. Micah had climbed on the table just as *Daed* walked into the kitchen. *"Nee,"* he said, scooping him up in his arms and tapping him on the bottom. "You know better than that." He set him down in his high chair, then sat down at the end of the table.

"There you are with those eggs." *Mami* took the basket from her. "What took you so long?"

"I . . . I . . ." Mary Beth didn't want to lie to her mother. She knew lying was wrong, and nothing good came from it. But she doubted her mother would appreciate that she'd wasted time staring at the sunrise.

"Never mind." *Mami* turned away and started cracking eggs into the pan on top of the gas stove. "Just set the table, please."

Mary Beth nodded, feeling guilty. She wished her mother wouldn't get upset so easily lately. Then again, Mary Beth had been wasting time. If she had come in right after gathering the eggs, her *mami* probably wouldn't be so upset.

She took the plates down from the cabinet and started setting the table. Caleb and Johnny plopped down in their seats, each boy flanking their father. Caleb and Micah were the spitting image of *Daed*. They had the same brown eyes. Their light brown hair was cut in the usual Amish style: bangs covering their forehead and touching their eyebrows, sides hanging over their ears.

She and Johnny, however, looked more like their mother; they had her blonde hair, although *Mami* and Johnny's hair was more straw-colored. Mary Beth's eyes were bluish-gray, but Johnny had the same brown eyes as her parents, and his black lashes were longer than hers. "His eyes are too pretty for a *bu*," she'd heard her grandmother say once. To make matters worse, her best friend, Katherine, had more than once mentioned how handsome they were. Katherine had a crush on Johnny. Mary Beth had hoped her friend's interest in Johnny would wane over time, but it hadn't in the past year. It was a sticky situation.

"*Danki*, Mary Beth." *Daed* gave her a small smile as she set his plate in front of him. She smiled back, feeling a little better. At least one of her parents wasn't put out with her this morning.

"There." *Mami* plopped a platter of fried eggs on the table, then wiped her hands on her apron. "Breakfast is ready. Johnny, stop flicking Caleb's ear and bow your head for prayer."

After silent prayer they passed the platter around, her mother taking the last egg. As Mary Beth bit into a piece of cold toast, her guilt returned. "I'm sorry, *Mami*. I won't be late again."

"Please don't be." She picked up her fork and started eating, not looking at anyone at the table. After a few bites she suddenly frowned. Mary Beth thought she even looked a little queasy.

"Hannah, are you okay?" Her father set his fork down and looked at her, worry on his face.

She nodded. "I'm fine, Daniel." She lifted another fork-ful of eggs to her mouth, but didn't eat them. Instead she dropped her fork and food on the plate, making a loud clat-ter. Pushing away from the table, she popped up and dashed out of the room.

"What's wrong with *Mami*?" Caleb asked.

Daed paused before he spoke, the worry on his face deep-ening. "She has a stomachache, Caleb. I'm sure that's it." He shoved away from the table. "Caleb, clear the dishes and keep an eye on Micah."

Caleb scowled but didn't say anything. Normally he would protest doing anything in the kitchen, but from their father's tone they could all tell he wasn't in the mood for arguing.

"Johnny, help me with the buggy. Mary Beth, you'll need to feed the pigs again."

Mary Beth nodded, hiding the urge to groan. The pigs again. But she was worried about *Mami*. And she suspected what might be wrong. Her mother couldn't be expecting another baby, could she? Mary Beth didn't think she could take another little brother. But she remembered how nau-seous her mother had been when she was pregnant with Micah. Maybe it was just a stomachache after all, like her *daed* said. She hoped that's all it was.

"I'll meet you outside, Johnny." *Daed* stood up and left the kitchen, just as he always did before going to work. But instead of heading for the back door, he went in the same direction her mother had gone, toward the back of the house where their bedroom and the second bathroom were.

Mary Beth started to go outside to do what her father had said when Caleb stopped her. "I'll do the pigs. You do the dishes and babysit."

"*Daed* said for you to do it."

Caleb scowled again. "He won't know the difference, just as long as the work's done."

"You better do what *Daed* says," Johnny piped in. He adjusted one of his suspenders over his shoulder. "He'll be mad if you don't."

"I don't wanna babysit him!" Caleb pointed at Micah, who had smeared egg yolk all over his plate with his fingers. "And I don't wanna do the dishes."

"You think I want to feed the pigs?" Mary Beth said, putting her hands on her hips.

"That's why we gotta trade."

"*Mami*'s already upset at me. I don't want to make *Daed* mad too."

"You won't." Caleb dashed out the door before Mary Beth could say anything. She turned to Johnny. "Do something before *Daed* gets back!"

"Like what? Caleb doesn't listen to anyone. You should know that by now." He walked toward the back door. "I'll keep an eye on him. I'm sure he can handle the pigs."

Mary Beth had to admit that she was glad Caleb had taken over the smelly job. Her brother was probably right—their *daed* wouldn't care who did what job, as long as the work was done. Grabbing a paper towel off the roll hanging near the sink, she wet it down, then went to Micah. She had just finished cleaning the egg off his face when her father walked in.

"Where's Caleb?" His eyes turned angry as they darted around the room.

"He's out with the pigs." Mary Beth bit the inside of her lip.

"I told you to do that." His eyes sparked with irritation.

Micah started to cry at the sound of their father's loud voice. Mary Beth picked him up and held him close. "Caleb wanted to do it."

"I gave you that chore for a reason." He ran a hand through his hair. "You're taller and can reach the latch to close the pen. I can't afford for those pigs to be getting out all the time." He frowned. "The next time I tell you to do something, Mary Beth, you do it. Understand?"

"But *Daed*, it was Caleb's—"

"Don't blame this on Caleb. You're the oldest. Your mother and I depend on you. I shouldn't have to wonder if you're going to do as you're told." He turned around and walked away.

Mary Beth's bottom lip trembled. Now both her parents were mad at her, and it wasn't even her fault. Well, not completely anyway. Why couldn't she do anything right?

Micah had stopped crying, and Mary Beth put him down. She gave him a wooden spoon to hold while she finished clearing the dishes on the table. Before long he was banging it against the leg of the table.

She had just started to fill the sink with hot soapy water when her mother walked in. Without a word she took the spoon from Micah and set it on the table, then picked him up. Mary Beth thought she would be mad, but instead she just sighed.

"*Danki*, Mary Beth." Micah laid his head on her shoulder. "I'm sorry for being short with you earlier. I didn't mean to snap at you."

"Are you feeling better?"

Her mother gave her a weary smile. "*Ya*, I am."

"Are you sick?"

Her mother paused for a moment, then looked away. "Possibly." But she didn't say anything else, just took Micah and left the room. Mary Beth frowned, still wondering what was going on.

As Mary Beth finished the dishes, she looked out the kitchen window and saw her father leaving in the buggy while Caleb chased Johnny across the front yard. A warm breeze blew into the window, and the sun was up in the sky now, warming the kitchen. After she wiped down the table, Mary Beth went into the living room. She saw her mother asleep on the couch, Micah playing with several wooden blocks on the floor beside her. It wasn't like her *mami* to take naps in midmorning. Usually she had already started working on her sewing.

"*Mami?*" Mary Beth nudged her gently on the shoulder.

Her mother's eyelids fluttered open. "Mary Beth?" She glanced around the room; then she sat straight up, wide-eyed. "What's wrong?"

"Nothing. I just wondered if you were okay."

Her mother adjusted her *kapp* and straightened the ribbons. "I'm fine. I just wanted to lie down for a few minutes before I started on those new winter coats for the Schlabach family."

"Can I help? Remember, you promised you'd show me how to sew the coats." Mary Beth knew how to sew a little, as most of her friends did. It would be a skill she'd need to master before she married. And even though marriage was a long way off, that didn't squash her desire to learn how to do more than repair her skirt hems or a rip in the seam of one of her brother's trousers.

"I know I did, but now's not a *gut* time." *Mami* rose from the couch, stepped over Micah and his blocks, and went to the wooden hope chest on the opposite side of the room, where she kept her fabric and sewing supplies. "I'm already behind on these coats."

"But I can help you catch up."

"I'll show you how soon. I promise." *Mami* pulled out the dark blue polyester fabric, a large pair of shears, navy-blue thread, and a tape measure. When she went to sit back down on the couch, Micah tossed one of his blocks, then stood up and went to Mary Beth, who lifted him in her arms.

"Mary Beth, please take him outside. And check on Johnny and Caleb—I haven't seen them since breakfast." She sighed. "I can only imagine what they've gotten themselves into."

Mary Beth nodded and did as she was told, even though she would have rather been inside with her mother than watching after her brothers. But arguing was out of the question, so she stepped outside and squinted in the bright light of the morning sun. Johnny and Caleb weren't in the backyard. She walked Micah to the tire swing attached to the big oak tree a few feet from the house. Micah climbed up and began to swing while Mary Beth looked more closely around the yard for her two other brothers. She didn't see them.

"Caleb? Johnny?" She glanced at Micah, who was happily singing as he swung back and forth in the tire. *He's okay*, she thought, *for a minute*. She left him and went to the barn. Maybe the boys were fooling around in there. As she neared, the scent of pig muck and horse dung made her wrinkle her nose.

"Johnny? Are you and Caleb in here?" The pigs started to oink and huddle against the wooden gate of their pen. "You've already been fed," Mary Beth said, walking past them. "Don't be so greedy."

She took another good look around the barn, but there was no sign of the boys. Knowing she had to get back to Micah, she turned around.

"Boo!"

Mary Beth jumped back, tripped over the hoe that someone had left in the middle of the barn floor, and fell down hard on her bottom.

"Gotcha!" Caleb and Johnny doubled over with laughter.

"That's not funny!" she shouted, her feelings hurting more than her backside.

"*Ya*, it is," Johnny gasped. "You should have seen your face." He put his palms against his cheeks and formed his mouth into an O shape. Then he started laughing again.

Mary Beth glared at him, and he stopped laughing. He walked over and held out his hand. "Here, I'll help you up."

She ignored him and stood by herself, then brushed the dirt from her dress. Her cheeks heated with embarrassment. Her brothers had once again made her the butt of their joke. Even though Johnny had tried to help her, she could still hear him and Caleb chuckling as she left the barn to check on Micah. At least she didn't have to worry about him scaring the life out of her.

But when she went to the oak tree, the tire swing was empty. Micah was gone.

"Micah? Micah!" When he didn't respond to her cries, she called for Caleb and Johnny.

They came running out of the barn. "What?"

"Micah's missing!"

"Naw, he's not," Caleb said. "He's got to be around here somewhere. Probably went back inside the house."

Hoping her brother was right, Mary Beth ran inside, calling Micah's name. Her mother was standing over the kitchen table cutting pattern pieces out of dark blue fabric. "Did Micah come in here?"

Mami put the scissors down. "*Nee.* He's supposed to be with you."

Fear rushed through Mary Beth. "I just left him on the swing for a minute—"

"You left him?" Her mother dashed out the back door. "Micah!"

Mary Beth followed. Johnny and Caleb stood by the swing, both of them looking upset.

"You two go to the back field and look for Micah." *Mami's* voice was laced with panic.

Johnny and Caleb bolted toward the field.

Mami looked at Mary Beth, her eyes fearful. "You check in the barn."

"But I was just there a few minutes ago. He's not in the barn."

"Then go look in the shed!" *Mami's* face turned white. "I'll check near the pond."

Mary Beth's fear rose. She hadn't thought about the pond, which was situated several yards beyond the house and out of view. What if Micah had wandered over there and fallen in? *Please, Lord, don't let Micah drown. I'm sorry I left him alone. I'll never do that again, I promise. Just keep him safe and help us find him.*

Mary Beth ran to the shed. The door didn't have a lock on it, and she thrust it open, narrowing her eyes as she peered into the cool darkness. "Micah?" She walked farther in, continuing to call his name, breathing in the earthy, stale air. Her father kept the gardening and yard tools in here, along with a large old cooler. Maybe her brother had climbed inside. She lifted the lid of the dingy white container, hoping to see his small body curled inside it.

He wasn't there.

She let the lid slam shut, then searched every corner of the shed. Still no Micah. Tears formed in her eyes. Where was he? This was all her fault. She shouldn't have left him alone. If something happened to him . . .

Shaking her head, she hurried out of the shed. She wouldn't have those thoughts right now. Instead she would focus on finding her little brother. Stepping out into the daylight, she called Micah's name one more time, but he didn't reply.

"Found him!" She heard Johnny's voice, far away.

Mary Beth followed the sound. She ran to the large field behind their house, her bare feet slapping against the grassy ground. The property next to theirs was owned by another Amish family, the Millers, who owned a blacksmith shop. The property wasn't fenced in; just a wide-open meadow separated their houses. Johnny was emerging from the tall grass, holding Micah's hand, the top of his brown head barely visible. *Mami* quickly joined them.

"*Gut* heavens, where have you been?" She scooped Micah up in her arms and kissed his forehead. The toddler put his finger in his mouth and leaned his head against her shoulder.

Mami turned, her eyes narrowing. "I told you to watch him, Mary Beth."

"I was, but you said to check on Caleb and Johnny too, and they were in the barn." Mary Beth twisted her fingers together. "Micah was on the swing, and I thought he would stay there. I didn't know he could climb down by himself."

"You should have taken Micah with you. Never, ever leave a child alone, Mary Beth. He could have fallen into the pond and—" She wiped her hand over her shiny eyes and blinked. "You're thirteen years old. I shouldn't have to tell you how to watch a *kind*." *Mami* pressed her lips to Micah's temple again. Without another word she went inside, leaving Mary Beth to wallow in her guilt.

"Now look what you did."

Mary Beth turned to Caleb, who was scowling at her. "I didn't do anything!"

"You lost Micah and now *Mami*'s mad. She'll probably be mad for the rest of the day." He kicked a pebble with his bare toe. "Thanks a lot, Mary Beth. You ruined our day."

She didn't have to put up with this. She felt bad enough without her siblings adding to her misery.

"Mary Beth—," Johnny started.

Not wanting to stick around to hear what he had to say, Mary Beth took off running as fast as she could. She had to get to her special place. She was halfway there when she slowed down, wiping the tears that had rolled down her cheeks. She stopped, gasping for breath.

"Mary Beth, wait up!" Johnny called out from behind her.

Mary Beth groaned. Why was he following her? Refusing to turn around, she started running again. But Johnny was faster and quickly caught up.

"Mary Beth, stop."

After running a few more paces, she slowed down, then came to a standstill. Turning, she looked at him, boiling mad, trying to catch her breath. "I don't care what you have to say. I know I messed up. Now leave me alone!"

"*Nee*, not until you tell me where you're going."

"None of your business."

"*Mami*'s gonna be mad you took off like this."

"Who's going to tell her?" Mary Beth glared at him.

Johnny just shrugged.

"*Mami*'s already mad, so it doesn't matter."

Johnny wiped his nose with the back of his hand. "So now you're gonna make her madder? That's not too smart."

"I don't care. Don't you get it? I just want to be alone!" She dashed off. She didn't care what he thought or even what her mother thought. She wanted to be by herself.

A few hours later Mary Beth opened her eyes. Her eyelids were sticky. At first she didn't know where she was—then she remembered what had happened that morning. She sat up, raised her arms above her head, and stretched. The last thing she remembered was running away from Johnny. When she'd reached the barn, she'd plopped down on her blanket and cried, then felt silly for acting like such a baby. She was thirteen, for goodness' sake! Way too old to be crying. But she couldn't help it. Almost losing Micah had scared her more than she would admit to anyone.

Straightening out her legs, she wondered how long she'd been asleep. The shadows in the barn told her it was late in the afternoon. *Uh-oh*. Dread pooled inside her, and at the same time her stomach started to growl. Not only was she probably going to get into trouble again, but she'd missed lunch. She would be glad when this horrible day was over.

She jumped up from her makeshift bed, not bothering to

straighten anything up. She was in a hurry to get home. But then she spied her juice boxes in the corner. The other day she had brought five—now there were only three! Although she didn't remember falling asleep, she definitely knew she hadn't had anything to drink. She knelt down and searched through the rest of her things. Maybe the extra boxes were hidden underneath something. After a few moments of searching, she realized they weren't.

She frowned, lost in her thoughts. First a mysterious button, then a bent page in her journal . . . now her juice boxes were missing. What was going on?

Standing up, she glanced around the barn. For the first time the cavernous space had lost its comforting appeal. She shuddered. Someone was watching her. She could feel it.

"Who's there?" she called out, walking the length of the dirt floor. "I know someone's here."

She heard a rustling sound outside. Rushing out the door, she ran around the back of the barn, expecting to find the spy. But nobody was there. *Great.* Now her imagination was running wild. She needed to get home before she lost her mind completely. She took a step backward.

Someone grabbed her arm.

Three

"Аhhhh!" Mary Beth screamed as she felt the hand on her arm, almost jumping out of her skin with fright. She looked into the face of her attacker, and her heartbeat slowed down a fraction. It was only her brother. The stray black-and-white dog trotted up right behind him.

"Johnny!" she sputtered. "Stop scaring me like that! You're not funny!"

"I wasn't trying to be." He let go of her arm and looked around, tipping his straw hat backward off his forehead. "So this is where you've been hiding out. The old barn." He turned to her. "I thought you didn't like getting dirty."

"What are you doing here?" Mary Beth ignored his comment. As if sensing her dismay, the dog walked over to her, licked her hand, then sat down beside her. She rubbed behind his ears, feeling calmer already.

"I followed you," Johnny said. "Wanted to see where you were running off to."

"Why? What do you care?"

He touched the splintered, graying wood, not looking her in the eye. "I was just curious. Seems like you've been disappearing an awful lot lately."

Mary Beth frowned, but some of her anger disappeared. A moment ago she had wanted to throttle her brother, but of course she never would. She'd been taught from an early age that hitting was wrong, and violence wasn't the Amish way. That didn't stop her brothers from playfully punching each other when they thought no one else was looking, but Mary Beth made sure she kept her hands to herself. Besides, deep down, she knew Johnny cared. He wouldn't have followed her out here if he didn't. That made her feel a little better.

Then she thought of something else. "Are you going to tell *Mami* and *Daed*?"

Johnny stared at her for a moment. She chewed on her fingernail, waiting for him to answer. "Please," she begged. "Don't. You know how much trouble I'll be in if you tell them."

He made his way around the barn to the front entrance and walked inside as if he owned the place. The dog joined him, following Johnny as if he were his master. Johnny looked around, nodding. "Sure is big in here. Wonder what kind of animals they had?"

"Horses and cows."

He looked at her "How do you know?"

"I don't. I'm just guessing. What else would you have in a barn?"

"Sheep? Goats? All kinds of animals. I can't believe anyone would let a nice barn like this go to waste. If this were
my barn"—Johnny looked around thoughtfully—"I'd have
the stalls set up over here." He pointed to the south side.
"Then I'd divide it down the middle and have the cows on
the other side, with a smaller section for the pigs. Maybe
add a goat or two. The chickens would have to fend for
themselves." Glancing down at the dog, he asked, "What
do you think?"

The dog barked his approval.

The more Johnny talked, the more irritated Mary Beth
became. Why wouldn't he give her a straight answer? He had
teased her in the past, but never about something this serious.
"Johnny, this is not your barn!"

"It's not yours, either. You know *Daed* told us to stay out
of here."

She cast her gaze downward. "I know."

"He'll ground you for the rest of the summer if he finds
out."

"I know." She looked up. "But you're not going to tell
him, are you?"

Johnny didn't say anything for a long moment, and with
each second of silence, Mary Beth knew her secret place
wouldn't be secret anymore. He would tell their parents, and
she would never be able to escape again. She went to her
private corner and started gathering her things.

"What are you doing?" he asked, looking surprised.

"Taking everything home." Her eyes burned as she picked

up her journal. She refused to cry in front of her brother, but she struggled to keep the tears from spilling.

"Why would you do that?"

She looked up at Johnny, only mildly puzzled by the surprised look on his face. "I won't be coming back here, so I need my stuff."

"Aw, Mary Beth, I ain't gonna tell."

Her eyebrows lifted. "You're not?"

"*Nee.*"

"Then what took you so long to answer me?"

"I was thinking." He shoved his hands in his pockets. "And this is what I came up with. We should share the barn. That half can be yours, and this half will be mine."

Mary Beth shook her head. She couldn't agree to those terms. "I'm not sharing this with you. I have to share everything else."

"You get your own room."

"That you and Caleb won't stay out of."

"Okay, you got me there. But we don't share clothes."

"Because *Daed* would have a fit if he saw you in a dress."

Johnny grinned. "Yup, he sure would. Not that I would want to wear one of those things anyway." He crossed his arms over his thin chest. "So—we're gonna go halfsies on the barn, *ya?*"

She shook her head. "*Nee.*" She couldn't give up her special place. She crossed her arms over her chest and stared him down.

Johnny arched his brow. "You don't want me telling *Mami* and *Daed*, do you?"

Shaking her head, she said, "Are you threatening me?"

He sighed and uncrossed his arms. "I don't want to tell, Mary Beth. But this barn's a really neat place. It's not fair that you have it all to yourself. We don't even have to be here on the same days. I'll make sure not to bug you when you're here."

She had to admit he was right. There really wasn't any reason they couldn't share it. She would still be able to spend time here alone, which was what she wanted. If Johnny told, she wouldn't have that at all. "Okay," she said, resigned. "You win."

Johnny let out a yell. "Yes! I can't wait to tell Dan and Nathan about this place."

"Now wait a minute," she said, shaking her head. "You can't tell *them* about the barn. People will find out, including *Mami* and *Daed*." Dan Miller couldn't keep a secret even if someone taped his mouth shut. She'd just given up half the barn to keep her secret, and now her brother was talking about revealing it to most of Middlefield, which is what he would be doing if he told Dan.

"You can't expect me to hang out here by myself."

"I do it all the time." She put down her journal. Maybe Johnny would realize how boring it would be for him here and decide not to come back. She saw the juice boxes again. Maybe this wasn't the first time Johnny had been out here after all. She faced him again. "And listen, I don't appreciate you stealing my stuff."

His mouth dropped open. "What are you talking about?"

"You took my juice boxes." She pointed to them lying on the ground.

"I did not!" He walked over to her corner and glanced down. "The boxes are right there. Besides, didn't you steal them from *Mami*? I'm sure she doesn't know you took them from home."

Mary Beth's cheeks reddened. He was right, but she wasn't about to admit it. "Then explain to me how I had five juice boxes, and now I only have three. Some of my other snacks are gone too."

"Maybe a mouse got them."

"Three granola bars?" She shot up and faced Johnny. "Tell me the truth, Johnny. You followed me here, then drank my juice and ate my snacks while I was sleeping."

"For the last time, Mary Beth, I didn't touch your stuff. I followed you here, but then I had to turn around and go back home because I heard Caleb calling me. You wouldn't want him coming out here, would you?"

She shook her head.

"So I went back home. I wasn't able to get away until a little while ago, and I came out here to let you know *Mami's* looking for you."

Oh no. "Why didn't you *say* something? How long ago?"

"About half an hour." Johnny's face turned white. "I kinda forgot."

"We have to *geh!*" She headed out the door, Johnny close behind.

"If you hadn't been blaming me for your missing juice—," Johnny said.

"Never mind that! Just hurry up! *Daed*'s probably home by now."

"Great! Now we'll both probably be in trouble."

She and Johnny left the barn and ran across the field toward home. They were halfway there when Johnny turned around. "Where's the dog?"

Mary Beth slowed a little and glanced around. The dog wasn't anywhere in sight. He must have left when she and her brother started arguing. "I don't know. I'm sure he'll show up again, but we have to get home now!" She quickened her steps, almost catching up to Johnny by the time they reached their property.

When they arrived, her father's buggy was parked in the yard. *Rats.* Dinner was probably on the table, and it was always her job to help prepare the meal and set out the dishes and silverware. Johnny looked worried too. Together they walked inside, silent, Mary Beth praying her parents hadn't already started the evening meal.

Everyone was already seated and eating. Neither their mother nor father looked up at them when they walked over to the table. Instead they continued to eat their supper of chicken and noodles. But it wasn't the silent treatment that worried Mary Beth the most. Caleb hadn't looked up from his plate at all, which was unlike him. Usually he had a smart remark for her or Johnny when they were in trouble. But this time he didn't say anything, just pushed a few noodles around on his plate. Micah peered over the rim of his cup, then set it down on the table and stuffed a noodle in his mouth, unaware of the trouble stewing all around him.

Without a word, Mary Beth went to sit down at her place at the table. She braced herself for the lecture to come. But when she pulled out her chair, she noticed there wasn't a plate set for her. Johnny didn't have one either.

"Supper is at six sharp," their father said, still not looking at them. "If you can't be here on time, you don't get any supper."

Mary Beth's stomach growled. Because she'd left home in the morning, she'd missed lunch too. But she knew better than to protest. Her father wouldn't back down on his word. She glanced at her mother, who continued to eat as if she and Johnny weren't even there.

"*Geh* to your rooms." *Daed* scooped up a forkful of noodles, then put them in his mouth, a tiny drop of gravy landing on his bearded chin. He picked up his napkin and wiped it away.

"But—," Johnny said, gripping the back of the chair.

"Your rooms. Now."

The twins ran upstairs. Mary Beth threw herself on the bed, her stomach growling in protest again. She was so hungry. And there would be no dessert tonight and no sneaking downstairs for a bite to eat. She'd have to wait for breakfast.

She sighed as she slipped into her pajamas. Then she

took another look at her button. She rubbed her thumb over the smooth metal. What if Johnny was telling her the truth about not taking her stuff? Deep down she knew he was. Her brother could be irresponsible, but he wasn't a liar. That meant someone else had recently been in the barn. A shiver passed through her. What if this button hadn't been left behind a long time ago, but in the past few days? Maybe the person who left it behind had also taken her crackers and juice.

She heard a knock on the door then and was relieved. Usually when she was in trouble, her *mami* would come up at bedtime and they would talk about whatever Mary Beth had done wrong. They had never gone to bed mad at each other. Now she could tell her mother she was sorry for being late and promise her it would never happen again. But when she opened the door, it wasn't her mother standing there. It was Johnny.

"What do you want?" She turned around and left the door open. Johnny walked inside.

"To tell you I'm sorry."

Mary Beth whirled around, surprised. "Sorry?"

"*Ya*. I should have told you *Mami* was looking for you right away. Then neither of us would be up here right now." His stomach growled loudly. "I'm starving. Now I wish I had eaten some of your snacks."

"You really didn't eat them? Or the juice?"

Johnny nodded. "I promise, Mary Beth. I didn't touch any of it."

Mary Beth sat down on her bed. "I believe you. It was *dumm* of me to accuse you of it. I'm sorry."

He nodded. "Okay."

"But if you didn't take the food, then who did?" She curled her fist around the button in her hand.

Johnny sat down beside her, the mattress sinking beneath his weight. He had taken off his hat, and his blond hair was matted down at the crown but flipped up over his ears.

"What's that?" he asked, pointing at her hand.

Reluctantly she opened it up. "A button."

He examined it for a moment. "Where did you get it?"

"The barn. I found it on the floor."

"Whose is it?"

"I don't know." She looked at her brother. "I think someone else knows about the barn, Johnny. We have to find out who it is."

Both Mary Beth and Johnny were grounded for the rest of the week. They were given extra chores, enough that they didn't have any time to spare. Every night, Mary Beth fell into her bed exhausted. She didn't even have the energy to draw in the journal she kept in her room underneath her bed. But the house was cleaner than it had ever been, and the barn and yard were now in perfect shape. There wasn't a weed to be found in the garden, either.

On their first day of freedom, *Mami* told Mary Beth that she had a doctor's appointment and was taking Micah and

Caleb with her. She would pay a Yankee to drive her and the boys because the doctor's office was too far for the horse and buggy to travel—about forty-five minutes away by car. Their family had several friends who weren't Amish who would take them and other Amish people to places they could only get to by car. *Mami* usually paid them something for their trouble and gas.

"I expect you and Johnny to behave while I'm gone," *Mami* said, pinning her black shawl around her neck and letting it fall over her shoulders. "I need to be able to trust you, Mary Beth. You too, Johnny."

Mary Beth nodded. "You can, *Mami*. I promise."

Johnny didn't say anything, but he also nodded his head.

"*Gut.* Now, I don't want you to go anywhere while I'm gone. Not even down the road to the Schrocks' house." *Mami* looked right at Johnny when she said that. "Stay put."

"Why? It's not like anything's gonna happen," Johnny said.

Mami peered at him, her lips lifting in a half smile. She put her black bonnet over her white prayer *kapp* and tied the ribbons underneath her chin in a neat bow. "Hmm. When have I heard that before, John?"

"You can believe it this time."

"Still," Mami said, "I want you to stay home." Johnny grinned at Mary Beth, then said, "Yes, *Mami*. "We'll be fine here."

But Mary Beth thought her brother was smiling a little too much. What was he plotting?

A car horn sounded outside, and Mary Beth handed Micah to her mother. "Caleb!" *Mami* shouted, then ruffled Johnny's hair. "Let's *geh!*"

Caleb dashed toward the door, skidding to a stop in front of the row of pegs where the hats and coats hung. He grabbed his yellow straw hat and plopped it on his head, then ran out the door. *Mami* and Micah followed.

Mary Beth could hear the sound of the car's tires on their gravel driveway as her mother and brothers left for the doctor. She looked out the window to see the white minivan drive down the road. Glancing up, she saw large gray rain clouds covering the sky. The air was hot and sticky even in the house. An afternoon shower would bring welcome relief.

Johnny came up behind her, looking over her shoulder. He glanced up at the sky, then said, "Let's *geh.*"

"What?"

"To the barn."

"Have you lost your mind? We just got ungrounded, and *Mami* said to stay put. We can't *geh* anywhere, especially not the barn."

"I thought that was your special place. Don't you miss it?"

"*Ya*, but not enough to get in trouble again." The truth was, ever since Johnny had discovered her secret, the barn wasn't that special anymore. She'd lost her hiding place where she could escape her annoying brothers and be alone with her journal and her dreams. Now that she had to share it with someone else, she wasn't in too much of a hurry to go back there. After the long week of being grounded and consumed with chores, she hadn't even thought about who might have also discovered her hiding place.

But Johnny wouldn't let it go. "*Mami* will be gone for a couple hours at least. That gives us enough time to investigate."

"Investigate what?"

"The mystery! We need to find out who's hiding in the barn."

Mary Beth walked away from the window. "It doesn't matter anymore."

"What do you mean it doesn't matter? Someone is trespassing in our barn." His brown eyes sparked.

"*Our* barn?"

"And we have to find out who it is."

Mary Beth went into the kitchen. There were a couple of dishes left over from lunch in the sink. She turned on the water, preparing to wash them. "You can *geh*. I'm staying here."

"You have to *geh* with me," Johnny pleaded.

"*Nee*, I don't. If you want to get in trouble again, *geh* right ahead."

"But . . ."

At the strange tone of Johnny's voice, Mary Beth shut off the water and looked at him. "But *what?*"

He glanced away. "I can't figure it out without your help."

Her eyebrows raised. Her brother had never, ever asked her for help before. He rarely asked anyone for help. It was a big deal for him to admit he needed her. "Why not?"

"You know the barn better than I do. You'd be able to tell if something was wrong or out of place."

She turned from him and stuck her hands in the soapy water, fishing for the dishrag she'd dropped in the sink earlier. But the last thing she wanted to do now was the dishes. Johnny's suggestion had brought back her curiosity about who was hiding in the barn. Now she was itching to find out—even if it meant she might get into trouble. She turned around and looked at him. "Promise we'll be back in an hour?"

Johnny's expression relaxed. "*Ya*. If we aren't, I'll wash the dishes for a week."

She couldn't resist that deal. Seeing Johnny wash dishes would be a sight to remember. Mary Beth smiled and nodded. "You bet. Let me finish here and we'll leave."

After the dishes were done, Johnny grabbed his hat and he and Mary Beth raced to the barn. Of course, he arrived before she did.

The clouds had grown slightly darker, the air heavier. Sweat trickled down Mary Beth's back and broke out on her face. They walked inside, and she welcomed the slightly cooler temperature. "What are we looking for?" she asked once she caught her breath.

"Clues," Johnny replied, barely sounding winded. He walked over to the far corner of the barn and looked behind an old, tilted hay bale.

Mary Beth followed her twin. "What kind of clues?"

"Any kind." He glanced at her over his shoulder.

"Shouldn't we be searching for something specific?"

"I don't know. I've never done this before. Just start looking."

Having no idea what to search for, she went to her

familiar corner to see if her possessions had been disturbed. At first she thought they hadn't, but then she noticed something. Her blanket had been folded before, and now it was wrinkled in a couple of places. "Found a clue!"

Johnny rushed up behind her. "You did? Where?"

"Here." She pointed at the folded blanket, then looked up at him.

He groaned. "That's not a clue."

"It is. I always fold my blanket before I leave."

"And it's still folded. How is that a clue?"

"You've seen me make my bed. I don't leave wrinkles."

He frowned slightly, shoving his hat back from his head. "You're right. You don't."

"Besides, last time I was here, I didn't fold my blanket." A shiver went through her. "Someone else must have used it and folded it up, thinking I wouldn't notice."

He knelt down beside her. "All right, so we have one clue. Anything else messed up?"

She picked up her journal, which was situated near the blanket. "I didn't mention this before, but I think someone's been reading this."

Johnny glanced down at the spiral notebook. "How do you know?"

"The corner of this page has been turned back." She flipped to the dog-eared page. "See?"

He peered at the nearly invisible crease in the corner. "Are you sure you didn't do it?" He moved to grab it from her, but she snatched it out of his reach.

"*Nee*, I didn't. At least I don't think I did." She clutched the journal to her chest so Johnny wouldn't get any funny ideas about reading her private thoughts.

"I guess we can call it a half clue, since you're not sure. Anything else?"

"I don't know. I haven't checked everything yet." She knelt down and tucked her journal under the blanket, then counted the juice boxes. There were still three remaining, the same number as before, plus the packet of crackers. She hadn't had a chance to bring any more food. Other than the wrinkled blanket, she didn't see anything else out of the ordinary.

"We need to check the rest of the barn. There's got to be something else here," Johnny said. But after a thorough search, they came up empty. There were no other clues to be found.

"Maybe whoever was here left," Mary Beth said. "He probably knows we're onto him by now."

"Or her. Or several people." Johnny hitched up his pants. His light blue, short-sleeved shirt was untucked in the front. "They might still be around here for all we know."

"I doubt it. I don't think we're going to find anything else." She went to the door of the barn and peeked outside. "We should probably go back, Johnny. If *Mami* catches us—"

"Don't worry, she won't. We'll be back in plenty of time." He walked past her and went outside, then turned around. "We need to search outside."

"But what if we don't find anything?"

"Don't tell me you're giving up." He pointed at her, shaking his head. "Never known you to give up so fast."

"I'm not giving up." She lifted her chin. "I just don't want to get in trouble. Again."

"I'm telling you, we won't. Now c'mon, let's search the outside."

Johnny's confidence was infectious, and Mary Beth followed him outside, hoping they would find another clue.

They walked around three sides of the barn, Johnny studying the ground as they made their way around the run-down building. "Rats," he said, putting his hands on his hips. He looked at Mary Beth. "You find anything?"

"*Nee.*" She shared his disappointment. Whoever had been here hadn't left any more evidence behind.

"Guess we better head back."

Nodding, Mary Beth turned on her bare heel and started to go back when Johnny's voice stopped her.

"Wait. Here's something." He motioned for her to come to him. "Can't believe we missed it before."

On the side of the barn right next to where the base of the wall met the ground, she saw a set of footprints. Indented swirls were evident in the soft dirt. "That's not from a work boot."

"*Nee.* More like a tennis shoe." Johnny put his bare foot next to the print, his long toes grimy from the dirt. "Just about the same size as mine."

"So another *bu* has been here, then?" Her eyes widened at the thought.

"Not necessarily. Could be a grown man. My feet are nearly as big as *Daed*'s, and this footprint is about his size." He looked at Mary Beth. "Someone has definitely been here, and recently."

"How do you know that's not from a long time ago?"

"It rained yesterday afternoon, remember?"

Mary Beth nodded. Even though she was sweating from the heat of the day, another shiver traveled down her spine. This was starting to get creepy. "Who do you think it is?"

"I don't know." Johnny studied the footprint a little longer. Then he looked at Mary Beth. "How long do you think we've been here?"

She rubbed her nose with the palm of her hand. "I'm not sure. Maybe a couple hours?"

He stood up. "Wow. I didn't think we were gone that long. We better get back."

"You want to go now? After we just found another clue?"

"We'll come back another time." He started to head toward the house, and for the first time she noticed a trace of worry on his face.

She hurried to catch up with him. "You don't think she's back yet, do you?"

"Nah." Then he looked at her, panic entering his eyes. Then they both burst into a run.

Just as they made it to the backyard, she heard the sound of a car pull into their driveway. "What if she sees us?" Mary Beth whispered even though her mother was several yards away.

"Just act natural," Johnny said out of the corner of his mouth. "For all *Mami* knows, we've been playing in the back-yard all afternoon."

"I doubt she'll believe that, Johnny. When was the last time we played together?" When they were younger they had been close and played together, but now that they were teens and Johnny had Caleb to hang out with, they rarely did anything together anymore.

"Can't remember, and it doesn't matter." He motioned for her to follow him to the swing set. "Follow me."

"The swing set?"

"It's the best I can do on short notice."

Mary Beth plopped herself on the wooden structure, which had been around as long as she could remember. She hadn't played on it too much in the last year or so, preferring to stay inside unless she was working in the yard or escaping to her secret place. But Johnny sat down next to her and started swinging, his expression happy, as if he didn't have a care in the world. She had to give him credit for a great performance. Following his lead, she took a deep breath and tried to relax, even though inside she was twisted up in knots.

From the swing set they could see *Mami* and the boys get out of the car and go in the house. Mary Beth had expected Caleb to come running outside and was surprised when he didn't. She was even more surprised when their *mami* started heading toward them.

"Oh no," she whispered to Johnny. "She knows."

"*Nee*, she doesn't." But he didn't sound confident, and Mary Beth noticed he had started swinging a bit faster.

As their mother neared, Mary Beth fought for calm. What was the worst thing that could happen? They'd get grounded again. But her mother would also be disappointed, and she'd lose her trust. That would be worse than getting in trouble.

When *Mami* stopped in front of them, both Mary Beth and Johnny slowed their swings, then finally stopped. She looked up at her mother. The bright sunlight was behind her, making it hard to see the expression on her face. Mary Beth squinted and gripped the thick metal swing chains.

Mami put her hands on her hips. "Well, now, what have you two been up to?"

Mary Beth wiped the perspiration from her top lip. "*Nix*," she said, dismayed at the tremor in her voice.

"Just swingin'." Johnny dug his bare heel into the dirt underneath the swing. "Swingin' and talkin'."

"I haven't seen you two do that in ages. Especially you, Mary Beth. I can't remember the last time you were on this swing set."

Mary Beth could feel her mother's gaze on her, even though she couldn't see her face clearly. She shielded her eyes with her hand and nodded.

"Did you finish your chores?" *Mami* asked.

"*Ya*," Mary Beth said.

Johnny twisted back and forth in the swing. "Me too."

Their mother dropped her hands. "I'm glad to hear it. *Danki* for doing what I told you to do. It's nice to know I can count on you two when I need to." As she started to turn, a smile formed on her face. "Keep on playing," she added. "You deserve some fun." With one last grin she walked back in the house.

"Whew." Johnny jumped out of the swing as soon as the door shut behind their mother. "That was close. I thought for sure we were sunk. I couldn't tell if she was upset or not."

"Me either." Relieved, she stood up from the swing. "She seemed happy that we're getting along."

"We've always gotten along, Mary Beth." Johnny took off his hat and ran his hand through his damp hair.

"Not as much lately."

He didn't say anything for a moment. "*Ya*, I guess you're right. But you're always reading, or writing in that journal of yours you keep under your bed—"

"How do you know my journal is under my bed?"

Johnny's face turned red. "Um, well, you see—"

"You've been snooping in my room!" Mary Beth took a step toward him. "That's not right!"

He held up his hands toward her. "It's not what you think. I wasn't snooping." He lowered his voice. "Caleb and I were upstairs rolling a couple of balls back and forth down the hall. It was raining and we were bored. One rolled into your room and under your bed. That's where I saw the journal. I promise."

Mary Beth let out a breath. "Okay. I'm sorry I accused you."

His blond brows furrowed. "That's not the first time

you've done that. Why do you keep thinking I'm out to get you?"

"I don't think that."

"You sure do act like it sometimes. Caleb's the snoop, not me."

She could read the hurt on his face. "I'm sorry, Johnny. I really am."

But he didn't say anything, only turned around and headed toward the house.

Mary Beth didn't follow him right away. She hadn't meant to hurt his feelings; she'd only been concerned with him reading her journal. Like the journal she kept in the barn, this one was filled with private thoughts and sketches, and the thought of one of her brothers reading it made her cheeks heat. He was right. While Johnny could be annoying at times, he had never messed with her things. Caleb had, more than once, but not Johnny. He was her twin, and she knew deep down she could trust him. Now she needed to show that.

As she headed toward the house, she saw the black-and-white dog approach from the direction of the field, holding something in his mouth. She knelt down as he came to her. He stopped a few inches away and dropped the object on the ground.

A crushed juice box.

She picked it up, then looked at the dog. He was sitting on his back legs, his pink tongue bouncing up and down as he panted. Examining the box, she saw the teeth marks embedded in the cardboard. At least she knew what happened to her juice boxes.

"*Gut bu.*" She patted the dog on the head and turned to catch Johnny before he went in the house. "Johnny, wait," she called out.

He stopped on the back deck and turned around, still looking irritated. "What?"

She ran up to him, clutching the juice box in her hand. "I really am sorry. I promise I'll trust you from now on."

His expression relaxed a bit and he nodded. Then he knelt down and started petting the dog. "You were right. He came back."

"And he brought this." She held out the juice box. "I guess we know what happened to my drinks."

Johnny took the box from Mary Beth. "He brought you this?"

"*Ya.*" So much for the big mystery. But then she remembered about the other clues in the barn. "It still doesn't explain the footprint, though. What should we do?"

He shrugged. "I don't know. I don't think there's anything we can do."

"But someone's hiding out there. Someone who doesn't want to be found."

"Maybe so. Or maybe he's behind it all."

The dog barked.

"The dog may have taken the food, but what about the button and footprint?"

"The property is owned by Yankees. Someone probably

came back to check on it." But Johnny didn't sound like he believed a word he was saying.

She moved to stand beside him on the back deck. "Let's look at the facts. No one's cared about that old barn for years. I remember *Daed* telling me about how shameful it was that someone would let that barn go to waste like that— and you said it too. Besides, if the owners showed up, they would have thrown all my stuff away."

"Okay, you have a point. But nothing we found proves that anyone is hiding there. Someone could have stopped by for a few minutes, saw the food and had a snack, then left. Don't you think that makes more sense than someone using that old place as a hideout?"

"I guess so . . ." She looked directly at him. "But I don't think you believe that."

Johnny opened his mouth to say something, then paused. He gave the dog one last pat and rose to his feet.

"Mary Beth!" her mother called from the back door. "Could you come inside, please?"

"Just a minute." She leaned over and whispered to her brother, "We'll talk about this later, *ya*?"

He nodded, and she left Johnny behind and joined her mother, who held the door open for her.

"Have a *gut* time with Johnny?" *Mami* asked as Mary Beth walked under her arm.

"*Ya*." She didn't look directly at her mother, afraid her face would give away the fact that she and Johnny had broken the rules again.

"*Gut.*"

Mary Beth looked at her mother. *Mami* was staring right at her, but her thoughts seemed elsewhere. Forgetting about the mystery at the barn for a moment, she asked, "Is everything all right?"

Her mother smiled. "Everything's fine, Mary Beth." Then she pulled out one of the kitchen chairs. "Have a seat. I'd like to talk to you about something."

Mary Beth sat, immediately curious. Her mother didn't look angry, so she couldn't know about her and Johnny sneaking away while she was gone. Still, she wasn't completely sure. Reaching for one of the black ribbons on her *kapp*, she started twisting it.

"I've got something to tell you, Mary Beth." *Mami* took her hand. "I'm pregnant."

Mary Beth's eyes widened. "You are?"

Mami nodded, her brown eyes shining. She let go of Mary Beth's hand and spoke. "I haven't been feeling very well lately. I've also been really tired. Now I know for sure—God has blessed us with another child."

Mary Beth didn't say anything for a long moment as she tried to figure out what to think. Micah was barely eighteen months. How could her parents even think about having another baby, especially when they had to work so hard to make ends meet as it was? And what if it was another *boy*?

"I know this is a surprise, Mary Beth, but it's God's will for us to have this child. Money will be a little tighter for us, but the Lord will provide. He always does. And I'm going to need your help now more than ever before."

Mary Beth brightened a bit. "I can help you with the sewing."

Mami shook her head. "I know that's what you want to do, but I'm going to have to take in as much sewing as I can before the *boppli* comes. Once the baby's here, I won't be able to sew as much. I appreciate you wanting to help me with it, but what I really need you to do is watch your brothers and take on more of the chores around the house while I sew." She leaned forward, and for the first time Mary Beth noticed the dark shadows under her eyes. "I promise, as soon as I can, I'll give you those sewing lessons. Okay?"

"Okay."

"*Danki, dochder.*" *Mami* sat back in her chair and let out a breath. The kitchen had grown hot during the afternoon, and her mother wiped her forehead with the back of her hand. "I'm really going to be depending on you these next few months. I haven't told your *bruders* yet. I wanted you to be the first to know. After your *daed*, of course."

Sitting up a little straighter in the chair, Mary Beth asked, "When will the *boppli* come?"

"January. So that gives us plenty of time to prepare." She reached for Mary Beth's hand again. "I'll be depending on you a lot, Mary Beth, especially with the household chores and taking care of the garden. Johnny will handle the animals and the yard work, like he usually does. He's been getting better about being more responsible. Caleb can help

him out too. But I know I can count on you." She squeezed
her daughter's hand. "I can't tell you how much that means
to me."

Mary Beth's initial disappointment over the news of the
baby was canceled out by the look of confidence in her
mother's eyes. Even after all the mistakes she'd made over
the past weeks, *Mami* still had faith in her. She didn't want to
let her down, not like she had lately. Her mother still trusted
her. Mary Beth wanted to be deserving of that trust.

"You can count on me, *Mami*." Mary Beth rose from the
chair, then pushed it back under the table, something her
mother and father were always getting on Caleb and Johnny
to do. "Do you want me to fix dinner tonight?"

"That would be great. I thought we might have sandwiches and eat outside tonight, along with the macaroni
salad I made yesterday. It will be cooler than eating inside."

Later that night Mary Beth put together a simple meal of
ham and Swiss cheese sandwiches, sweet pickles, the macaroni salad, and some chocolate oatmeal cookies she didn't
have to bake, which were really easy to make. After everyone
ate, Mary Beth settled on the front porch swing with a book
while the rest of the family stayed in the backyard and played.
She was just getting into the story when she heard a clicking
sound against the wooden boards of the porch. Glancing up,
she saw the black-and-white dog coming toward her.

Mary Beth set down her book and motioned for the dog

to come closer. She leaned down and stroked his head. His fur was thick and soft, but now he needed a bath and a good brushing; he had dirty paws and there were brambles stuck in the fur around his ankles. A bath would also take care of the strong doggy smell.

But she didn't care if he was dirty or smelly. She moved off the porch swing and sat right beside the dog.

"What are you doing?"

Mary Beth looked up to see her father standing over her, a frown on his face. "It's okay, *Daed*." The dog licked her hand. "He's very gentle."

"Do you know who he belongs to?"

She shook her head.

"Then he's a stray. What did your *mami* and I tell you about stray animals?"

"To stay away from them. But he's different. He helped us round up Hambone when he got out. He's really gentle. Plus look how healthy he is. I'm sure he belongs to someone nearby."

Her father crouched down. The dog immediately got up and went to him, then lay down in front of *Daed* and rolled over.

Daed chuckled and rubbed the dog's white stomach with his good hand. His injured hand lay limply on his knee. "I see what you mean. He probably does belong to someone." He gave the dog one last rub, then stood up. The dog flipped over and sat. "I still want you to be careful around him."

"I will, *Daed*."

"And make sure Micah doesn't go near him. He might pull on his tail or ears and make him angry. Understand?"

She nodded, and her father paused. "Did you need me?"

He shook his head. "*Nee*. Just wanted to see where my girl was." Grinning, he reached down and touched her *kapp*. "Making sure you were okay. *Mami* said she told you about the *boppli*."

Mary Beth stood and looked up at her father. He had taken off his hat, revealing the gold streaks in his brown hair. His hair always lightened up in the summer. "She did. And I promised her I'd help out."

He smiled, the dimple on his left cheek deepening. "I never had a doubt about that. You already help out a lot as it is, and we're both grateful."

Happiness flowed through her as she took in her father's proud smile.

"Why don't you come join the rest of us? Caleb and Johnny set up the volleyball net. I could use you on my team."

"But what about your hand?"

"Don't worry about that. I've gotten really good with my left hand." He lifted it up and swiped at the air. "What do you say? I think we can beat them."

Although she didn't play volleyball very often, she was eager to be on her father's team. "All right," she said, and they headed for the backyard. The dog immediately started to follow.

"Wonder what his name is?" her *daed* said, glancing over his shoulder at the animal.

"I don't know. He doesn't have a collar or tag. But he looks like a Roscoe to me."

Her father arched a brow. "Roscoe? Hmm, sounds *gut* enough. Probably won't answer to it—not that it matters, especially if he has his own home."

Mary Beth looked down at Roscoe, who was trotting beside her. She didn't want him to leave, but she wouldn't want him to stay if he belonged to someone else. If he were her dog, she'd be upset if he was missing. "Maybe we should ask around and see if anyone has lost a dog."

"That's a *gut* idea. I'll mention it at work tomorrow, and on Sunday we can put the word out." They had reached the backyard, and *Daed* put his hand on her shoulder. "Now, let's put Caleb and Johnny in their place. They're a little too confident right now."

They played for an hour, with *Mami* and Micah watching. Her father had been right—he was good at using his left hand, and they barely beat Caleb and Johnny. After promising them a rematch another time, they all went into the house and prepared for bed. Mary Beth was tired but happy.

She changed into her white, short-sleeved nightgown and crawled under the sheet. Night had fallen, and with it came the evening music of chirping crickets and croaking bullfrogs. Her mind mulled the day's events—the clues she and Johnny had discovered at the barn, the news about the baby, the return of Roscoe, who as far as she knew was still in the yard. Before going to bed she had left a bowl of water out for him. But while she was glad Roscoe kept coming around and she was getting used to the idea of *Mami* having another baby, her thoughts were centered on the mysterious person who had been in the barn. Because deep down she knew that was the truth—someone else knew about the old barn. Problem was, she didn't know what to do about it.

Her eyelids grew heavy with sleep. Just as she was about to drift off, she sensed a fly on her shoulder. She brushed it away and rolled onto her side, pulling her sheet up to her chin and closing her eyes again. A second later something nudged her harder. Rolling back, she opened her eyes. A shadow stood over her bed. She opened her mouth to scream—but a hand smothered her face.

Four

"BE QUIET!"

Mary Beth's eyes grew round as she looked up into Johnny's face. *"Whmf arf ymf doif?"*

"What?"

She yanked down on his arm. "What are you doing?" she whispered fiercely.

"Trying to keep you from waking up *Mami* and *Daed*."

She sat up in her bed. "What are you doing in my room? And for the last time, stop scaring me!"

"I didn't mean to scare you." He squatted down at the side of her bed. "Honest. Not this time, anyway."

"Then what do you want?"

"We need to go to the barn."

"What?"

"I said we need to go to the barn."

"Now?"

He nodded, his face barely visible in the dimness of the

room. Outside, a full moon cast a silvery glow into the bedroom, but the light would only last for so long. Johnny sniffed, then wiped his nose with the back of his forearm. She could tell his allergies were acting up. "It's the only way we're going to catch whoever's staying there."

She flopped back down on the bed, the back of her head hitting the pillow. "You're *ab im kopp*, Johnny. We've already snuck out to the barn once; now you want to do it again? Do you want to spend your entire summer grounded?"

"We won't get caught."

"How do you know?"

He paused, not saying anything for a moment.

She sat back up. "How do you know, Johnny?"

"Because I, um . . . I just know."

Mary Beth gasped. "You've snuck out before?"

He nodded. "More than once. And no one's ever found out. Trust me, they won't this time."

"Why would you sneak out?"

He hesitated for a moment. "It's kind of silly, but sometimes I have trouble sleeping. So I'll go outside when it's a clear night and count the stars."

"You count stars?"

"You should try it sometime. It works."

She bit her lower lip. She didn't want to talk about counting stars. She wanted to find out why Johnny kept waffling back and forth about the mystery in the barn. "What made you change your mind?"

"What?"

"Earlier you weren't sure about this. Now you're sneaking out in the middle of the night to find out who he is. I'm confused."

"I've had some time to think about it, and I figured you're right." Johnny sat on the edge of her bed. "Look, this thing will keep bugging me until I find out who it is. Don't tell me you haven't been thinking about it too."

"I have. But I wasn't going to sneak out in the middle of the night to find out."

"This is the best chance we'll have to catch whoever it is in the act. But we don't have all night. If you're coming with me, then we need to *geh* now."

Torn, she tried to figure out what to do. She wanted to go with Johnny—but she didn't want to risk getting in trouble and, worse, disappointing her parents. They had just said how important it was that they could rely on and trust her, yet here she was, close to betraying that trust. But if her parents didn't know she had snuck out, then they wouldn't be mad at her, right?

"Mary Beth." Johnny's tone was urgent. "Are you coming or not?"

Her curiosity overriding her better judgment, she threw off the sheet and clambered out of bed. "I'm coming. Just wait a sec. I gotta change clothes."

He looked at her. "Wear what you have on. I didn't change."

She glanced at his white T-shirt, pants, and bare feet. Other than not wearing a regular shirt, he didn't look much different than he normally did. She, however, was in her night gown, and she wasn't about to go outside like that. "Out," she shooed him away, still whispering. "I'll only be a minute."

"Meet me in the kitchen. Don't take forever!"

She quickly found her dress and slipped it on, then took a rubber band and pulled her waist-length hair into a ponytail. She should put on her *kapp*, or at least a kerchief, since Amish girls and women never left the house without their heads covered. But she didn't have time. She crept out of her bedroom and tiptoed down the stairs, her palms sweating, already starting to regret her decision. Yet she couldn't turn back now. She had to know.

When she walked into the kitchen, she saw Johnny's shadowy figure standing by the back door. She could barely make out him motioning her toward him. When she stood next to him, he put his finger to his lips. "Shh."

"I'm not saying anything," she whispered back.

"Now you are, so be quiet." Slowly he pushed on the back door, pausing when the hinges creaked. Mary Beth sucked in her breath. They froze in place, waiting to see if one or both of their parents would come downstairs and catch them in the act. When neither of them did, Johnny shoved the door open all the way, then pushed Mary Beth out onto the back deck. She half expected Roscoe to be there, but he'd disappeared again.

"Hey!" she whispered. "Stop pushing."

"Sorry. We needed to get out fast." He flew down the five wooden steps and started to run.

Quickly she followed, and they both sped off for the barn, the moonlight illuminating their way.

When they reached the barn, Johnny pulled out a small flashlight and flicked it on, directing the beam at the barn entrance. He turned to Mary Beth. "You go first."

She gaped. "Why me? This was your idea in the first place."

"But it's your barn."

"We're sharing it, remember?" She paused. "You're not chicken, are you?"

"*Nee*, of course not." He shone the light in her face, blinding her for a moment, before pointing it back at the barn.

"Thanks a lot." Spots danced in front of Mary Beth's eyes, and for a moment they were the only thing she could see. "If you're not scared, then go inside already."

"Fine." He stepped forward, but not with his usual enthusiasm. Johnny's reaction made Mary Beth's nerves spike. She couldn't remember the last time Johnny had been afraid of anything.

After taking one more hesitant step, he reached out for her. "C'mon," he said, tugging on her wrist and dragging her behind him. "We'll both go in together."

She let Johnny lead her inside. Normally she wasn't afraid of the dark. She was used to it—her family, like all Amish, didn't use electricity. At night they used battery- and gas-operated lamps or flashlights, sometimes only the pocket-sized ones that didn't give off much light.

But tonight was different. Even though they had Johnny's flashlight and the moonlight outside, nothing calmed her nerves. A place that seemed welcoming during the day had taken on a spooky appearance at night. The crickets and bullfrogs were noisier, and out of the corner of her eye, she kept thinking she saw something moving around . . . but when she turned her head to get a better look, there was nothing there.

"This is a bad idea, Johnny," she whispered as they walked into the barn. When he didn't say anything, she knew he agreed. Still, neither of them turned back.

Johnny moved the flashlight's beam around the barn, pointing it in corners. A flash of movement made Mary Beth jump. She gripped her twin's arm. "What was that?"

"A mouse," Johnny said. "I think."

"You think?"

"*Nee, nee,* I'm sure."

But she thought she heard her brother gulp.

For a few seconds they shone the light around the barn, searching for anything different than what they'd noticed earlier that day. "No one's here," Mary Beth said. "And from the looks of things, I don't think anyone has been here since this morning."

"I think you're right." He looked at her. "We should head back."

Those were the words Mary Beth was waiting for. She spun around on her heel, the skin of her foot rubbing against the dirt and strands of old straw, and headed for the barn door. The sooner she was home and in her bed, the better. Fear had finally conquered her curiosity.

Then, out of the corner of her eye, she saw some-thing move—this time for sure. She reached for Johnny's flashlight.

"Hey," he said as she pulled it out of his grasp. "Whatcha doing?"

"There's something over there."

"A mouse. I already told you that."

"It's not a mouse." She shone the light on the stack of hay bales, slowly moving toward it.

Johnny walked directly behind her. "I don't see anything."

"Hush!" She moved closer, switching the flashlight to her left hand as she tried to see what was behind the bales. Her hand trembled, and she hoped Johnny wouldn't notice. She didn't want her brother to know she was getting scared. When they were a few inches from the stack, she moved to the left side. "I know you're back there," she said.

Except for Johnny's breathing behind her and the sound of her heart beating in her ears, she didn't hear anything.

"There's nothing there." Johnny moved to take the flash-light from her.

"Stop it!" she exclaimed.

"It's my flashlight."

"But I need it."

"Give it back," he said.

"*Nee*. Not until I'm done with it."

"I want it back now—"

Achoo!

Mary Beth and Johnny stood still, Mary Beth's arm in the

air as she fought to keep the flashlight from Johnny. They both looked at the hay bales.

"Did you sneeze?" Johnny asked.

She shook her head. "Did you?"

"*Nee*."

Her adrenaline spiked. "I told you there was something over there."

"Okay, you were right." Catching her off guard, he plucked the flashlight from her grip and pointed it back at the bales. He slunk over to the stack with quiet, stealthy steps.

Suddenly something sprang out from behind the hay bales, knocking Mary Beth over. She landed hard on the ground. She heard her brother shout, then take off running, leaving her alone in the barn. She scrambled to her feet, trying to get her bearings. Thin slivers of moonlight shot through the gaping slats in the barn, and when her eyes adjusted she was facing the entrance, so she ran outside.

When she stepped out onto the cool grass, she looked around. Nothing. Then she heard her brother yell, "Stop!"

She ran around to the other side of the barn. Johnny was holding his flashlight toward the ground, the beam of light aimed at something on the ground. Or someone, she realized as she neared. She squinted, struggling to make the person out. It was a boy, not much older than she and Johnny.

"Don't run," Johnny said, moving slowly toward him. "We're not gonna hurt you."

The boy shrank back from the light, shielding his eyes.

Mary Beth moved to stand by Johnny. Here she could get a better look. The stranger had shaggy brown hair that hung over his eyes and touched the collar of his sweatshirt. At least she thought it was a sweatshirt. She could only see him from the shoulders up. But from his hairstyle she could tell he wasn't Amish.

"Who are you?" Johnny asked.

"I can't see!"

"Tell me who you are and I'll put down the flashlight."

Mary Beth noticed an edge in Johnny's voice. He wasn't playing around.

"Put down the flashlight and I'll tell you who I am."

"How do I know you're not going to run off?"

The boy held up his hands. "Where am I going to run? There's nowhere to go. You'll just tackle me again anyway."

"I didn't tackle you; I was just keeping you from running away." Johnny angled his flashlight away from the stranger.

Mary Beth heard him jump to his feet. True to his word, he didn't run off.

"Why are you staying in the barn?" Johnny asked.

The boy shrugged. "I didn't know it belonged to anyone. I thought it was abandoned."

"It's not anymore. Me and Mary Beth share it."

"Sometimes," she added. She stepped toward him, her fear suddenly disappearing. "I'm Mary Beth Mullet, and this is my brother Johnny."

"I don't care who you are or whose barn it is. I needed a place to stay for a while."

"So you're the one who's been taking my food and juice," she said.

Johnny flashed the light at the boy again, who was looking down at the ground, his greasy hair hanging down around the sides of his face like a dirty curtain. He didn't respond.

"If you saw the stuff inside, how could you think it was abandoned?"

He shrugged again. "I don't know. I never saw either of you two here before. I usually only come here at night."

Mary Beth's curiosity grew. "Where do you go during the day?"

"Here and there."

"Where do you live?"

He looked directly at her. "You're nosy, you know that? Both of you are."

"We have a right to be when you're trespassing," Johnny said.

Mary Beth was about to say they were all three trespassing, but she thought better of it. A bug buzzed around her ear. She swatted at it. "We should go inside the barn," she said. "We can talk in there."

"Who said I wanted to talk to you?"

His mean tone hurt her feelings, but she wasn't going to show it. "Fine. Go ahead and get bitten by bugs. See if I care. But I'm not standing out here anymore."

"Good. Both of you go home and leave me alone."

"Wait a minute." Johnny took a step forward. "Why don't *you* go home? This is more our barn than it is yours."

"Whatever." He turned to leave, but Mary Beth stopped him.

"Wait." She took the flashlight from Johnny and walked toward the boy. Her nose wrinkled as she got close to him. He smelled like he hadn't taken a bath in a long time. She flashed the light on his body. He was definitely a Yankee. Why did he have on a sweatshirt in the middle of summer? His jeans were dirty, torn at the knees and covered in green grass stains. He wore tennis shoes that might have been white at one time but were now gray and covered with dirt, the ends of the shoelaces frayed and coming apart. Even through the jeans and sweatshirt she could tell he was thin. When she turned the light so she could see his face, she noticed the sweat and grime covering it.

"Where did you say you lived again?"

"None of your business." He turned away.

"Do your parents know where you are?"

He faced her again. "Do yours?"

"*Ya*," Johnny said.

"Yeah, right. Like your parents let you run around in the middle of the night."

Johnny lifted his chin. "They do."

"Johnny, why are you lying to him?" Mary Beth gave her brother a disgusted look.

"Knew it." The boy wiped the back of his dirty hand over his sweaty forehead. Then he slapped at a bug that landed on his cheek. "Go back home before you get in trouble."

"What will you do?"

He looked at Mary Beth. "Don't worry about me. I can take care of myself."

"*Ya*, we can tell," Johnny said sarcastically.

Mary Beth didn't understand why her brother was acting so strange all of a sudden, telling lies and being mean. "Johnny, that's not nice."

"He's stealing our food, Mary Beth."

"My food," she corrected. She glanced back at the boy, holding the flashlight up a little higher. "He's right. Why did you take it?"

"Look, I'll pay you back. Not a big deal."

"Okay," Johnny said, stepping closer to him. He held out his hand. "Pay us back."

"I said I'd pay *her* back." He looked directly at Mary Beth, as if daring her to ask him for the money.

At that moment she saw something in the boy's eyes. Beneath his tough talk and emotionless face, she realized he was scared. She also realized he couldn't pay her back. From his ragged appearance and the fact that he was stealing food, she knew he didn't have any money. "Are you living in the barn?"

He shifted from one foot to another, glancing away, then looking back at her. "No."

"You're lying."

"Am not."

"I can tell you are."

"Let's *geh*, Mary Beth." Johnny snatched the flashlight from her and started to walk away. "He said he can take care of himself."

Mary Beth followed Johnny a short distance away from the boy. "We have to help him," she whispered. "Can't you see he's all alone?"

"He never said that."

"He didn't have to. I can tell."

"Doesn't matter."

"How can you say that?"

Johnny stopped and turned around, keeping the flashlight pointed at the ground. "This is none of our business."

Mary Beth clenched her fists. "You're the one who wanted to find out who was sneaking into the barn. Now that we have, you just want to leave him alone?"

"What can we do? He doesn't want our help."

"So that means we don't try? You know that's not right."

"Then what should we do?"

"First we have to find out who he is and where he lives. Or where he's supposed to be living." She took the flashlight from Johnny again, turned around, and headed back to where they had been standing. When she didn't see the boy, she said, "He must have gone back to the barn." Not waiting for Johnny, she walked inside and shone the flashlight around.

The boy was gone.

The next morning Mary Beth woke up early as she normally did, but she was still tired. She and Johnny had searched for the boy for a short time, but eventually they gave up. They had snuck back into the house just as easily as they had escaped, much to Mary Beth's relief. But she had tossed and turned all night, thinking about the stranger. She didn't even know his name.

Why was he staying in the barn? Had he run away from home? She assumed he had, even though she couldn't be sure. She couldn't imagine what it was like not having a bed to sleep in or meals to eat, even though she silently complained about eating the same simple meals all the time. A person couldn't survive on just juice and crackers. And from how thin he looked, she knew he had to be hungry.

She also couldn't imagine not having a home or parents who loved her. Even if something did happen to them, she had several aunts, uncles, and cousins she could live with. And if for some reason they couldn't take her or her brothers in, someone else in the community likely would. No one would let children, much less a single child, go without.

As she got dressed, she knew she'd have to go back to the barn and find him again. She doubted the boy would be there, but she could at least help him by leaving him some more food. But that would be hard, because it wasn't like her family had a lot of food to spare.

Maybe she should tell her mother about him. Yet if she did, then she'd get in trouble for going to the barn in the first place. And what if he'd left for good now? She'd get grounded for no reason.

No, there was only one thing she could do: sneak back to the barn again and see if he would show up. If he did, she'd try to talk to him again. At least she would convince him to tell her his name.

She headed downstairs and ran into Johnny on the landing. He looked as bleary-eyed as she felt and walked toward the kitchen without saying anything. She watched him, wondering what was going on. He was acting just as strangely this morning as he had last night.

When she went into the kitchen, Johnny wasn't there. Her mother was awake and looking better than she had in days. *"Guten morgen*, Mary Beth."

"Are you feeling better, *Mami?*"

"This morning I am." She smiled. "Caleb and Micah are out with your *daed* feeding the pigs. Micah wanted to watch. I asked Johnny to get the eggs this morning. Would you like to make chocolate chip muffins for breakfast?"

"Sure." Mary Beth smiled. She didn't mind cooking. It was much better than cleaning or watching her brothers. She loved chocolate, and chocolate chip muffins were her favorite. She gathered the ingredients to make the muffins—flour, baking powder, sugar, and chocolate chips from the pantry, and milk, eggs, and butter from the cooler downstairs. In the summer they kept food that needed to be cold in two large ice chests in the basement. In the winter they kept the ice chests outside on the back porch, especially in January and February, when it was almost always freezing out.

It didn't take her long to get the muffins in the oven and set the table.

Johnny came inside carrying a bowl filled with brown eggs. She glanced up at him as he handed the eggs over to their mother.

"Make sure you wash your hands," *Mami* reminded him.

As he washed them in the kitchen sink, Caleb burst into the kitchen.

"Shoes off, Caleb," their mother said, pointing at him.

Caleb turned around and kicked off his shoes, leaving them on the back porch. Then he headed for the sink just as their father and Micah came in. *Daed* set Micah in his chair, then went and stood by *Mami*, who was scrambling eggs.

"You smell like pig!" she said, but in a good-natured way.

Daed chuckled. "Glad to see you in a *gut* mood this morning, Hannah."

Mary Beth was glad to see her mother in a good mood too. With the sunlight streaming through the window, the scent of chocolate chip muffins in the air, and her parents happy, Mary Beth couldn't help but smile.

She placed the last fork on the table just as the timer went off. Her mother bent down and pulled out the muffins, placing the hot pan on a quilted pot holder. Mary Beth watched the steam rising from the muffins, her thoughts going to the boy in the barn again. Did he have anything to eat for breakfast this morning? Here they never went hungry, even though it seemed like they didn't have very much to eat. Still, she knew it was more than he had.

"Mary Beth," her mother said, intruding on her thoughts. "Breakfast is ready."

Once everyone was seated, they all bowed their heads in silent prayer.

Please, Lord, be with the boy we met last night. Keep him safe, and don't let him go hungry for long. Show me how I can help him. Amen. Mary Beth raised her head.

Daed passed around the platter of eggs. "You're awfully quiet, *sohn*," he said as he handed the large white platter to Johnny. "That's not like you."

Johnny scooped a spoonful of eggs, then passed the plate to Mary Beth. "Don't have much to say today."

"You also didn't take much food." *Mami* frowned. "Are you feeling all right?" She glanced at *Daed*. "Does he look sick to you?"

Daed stared at Johnny for a moment, then shook his head. "*Nee*, just tired. You didn't sleep well last night?"

Johnny shrugged, keeping his head down. "I slept okay."

"Daniel, feel his forehead, see if he's hot."

His father stretched out his hand, and Johnny ducked away. "I don't have a fever. I'm fine."

"But—," *Mami* started.

"If the *bu* says he's fine, he's fine." *Daed* ate the last bite of his eggs, then grabbed a muffin off the plate with his good hand. "I've got to *geh* to work. Caleb, help me hitch up the horse."

Caleb shot out of his chair and headed out the kitchen door. Their father said good-bye to the rest of the family, then followed Caleb.

Mami dabbed at her mouth with her napkin. "I cut out

the pieces for a new coat yesterday, and I want to start sewing on it. I'll take Micah with me into the living room. He can play while I sew. Mary Beth, would you mind taking care of the dishes, please?"

"*Ya, Mami.*" Mary Beth cleared the table as everyone left the kitchen. She washed the dishes, saving the muffin pan for last. There were two muffins left. Normally she would put them on a separate plate and leave them out for anyone who wanted to snack on them later. But instead she found a plastic baggie and placed the muffins inside. She went to the pantry and put them behind a large canister of oatmeal. They would be safe there until she could get them later. Then she went back to wipe down the table.

Her family didn't have much, that was true. But what they could spare, she would take to the boy.

The sound of roosters crowing in the distance woke up Sawyer Thompson. He felt something warm against his body. He looked to see the black-and-white dog who always kept him company at night. He stroked the dog's neck, then sat up and rubbed his eyes. He looked around, surprised to find himself in the middle of a field. To his right was the barn, the place where he had spent every night of the last two weeks. But last night he'd been discovered. And as the two kids who found him had argued with each other, he had run and hidden in the tall field grass. He must have fallen asleep while he was waiting to make sure they had left and weren't coming back.

He glanced over the field again, making sure no one was around. Satisfied, he stood up, the dog doing the same. His legs and arms itched, and he started scratching. When he pulled up the leg of his ripped-up jeans, he groaned. Tiny red bumps had popped out all over his skin. Mosquito bites. They must have bitten him while he was sleeping. Not that it mattered, because they usually got him when he was in the barn too.

Scratching his cheek, he headed back to the barn, forgetting about the mosquitoes and thinking about his growling stomach. He was starving, and although he knew he should find another place to stay, the truth was he couldn't. This was his only hiding spot, the only place he'd been sure he'd never be discovered. At least up until last night. Over the past week he'd managed to sneak into a few unlocked root cellars when no one was looking and steal some of the vegetables and apples—only a few, so no one would notice. He'd also found a small creek nearby and had been able to drink the water without getting sick, at least so far. But the old barn was his only shelter.

He entered the barn, grateful for its coolness. He went to the corner and plopped down on the folded blanket, the dog settling beside him, panting. Even though he had slept, he was still tired. And hungry. He saw the packet of crackers and started eating them, shoving them in his mouth, then handing a couple to the dog, who wolfed them down just as fast. Now that they knew he was here, it didn't matter if he made a mess or not, or even if he ate and drank everything.

He'd have to leave now, even though that wasn't what he wanted. He'd planned to stay here awhile until he figured out what to do next.

But then, Sawyer was used to everything going wrong. Nothing ever turned out the way he hoped it would.

The dog suddenly stood up and ran off, as he usually did during the day. Sawyer wasn't concerned; he'd see him again tonight. Flopping over, he slid his hand underneath the blanket and pulled out a small notebook. The word *Journal* was written on the light blue cover. As he had done since he'd first discovered the journal a few days ago, he flipped it open, reading the pages with interest, and with more than a little guilt. The journal most likely belonged to that girl. Mary Beth, he thought her name was. He'd first started reading it out of sheer boredom, but it wasn't long before he found himself interested in what she'd written and sketched on the pages. From the journal, he knew she could draw well, she had three brothers she didn't like at all, and there was a boy named Christopher she did like, then didn't, then liked again, then finally didn't. Girls. Who could figure them out?

Even though he didn't care about Christopher or her brothers, he was interested in her pictures. Pencil sketches of landscapes, of men dressed in funny clothes and hats working in a field, of women sitting around a large table sewing on a big blanket. He'd never seen anything like the people she depicted in the pictures, except maybe in his history book last year when he was in eighth grade.

He stared at one of the pictures, this one of three kittens

sitting around a saucer of milk. Just looking at the pictures gave him a sense of peace. Looking at the milk was also making him thirsty. He spied the juice boxes but didn't drink them. He would need them later, if they were still here. Now that he had been discovered, the kids might come back and take everything away. Worry wound through him. As he did every single day, he wondered if he would find enough to eat and drink to keep him going until the next day. His stomach growled. It had been a long time since he'd had a real meal. Or slept in a real bed.

He shut the journal and tucked it back under the blanket, fighting the frustration rising inside him. Would anything be right again? Somehow he doubted it.

Five

MARY BETH spent the rest of the day watching Micah and weeding the garden. It was nearing the end of June, and she had to make sure weeds didn't grow and choke the tender new plants. She could imagine how the garden would burst with fresh vegetables in a month or so. The tomato plants would be ready, filled with plump, red tomatoes. There would be green beans, yellow summer squash, and sweet peas. They would have plenty of vegetables to can for the winter, as long as she kept the weeds away.

Throughout the day she couldn't stop thinking about what happened last night. Johnny had left with Caleb to help one of their Yankee neighbors down the road clean up his yard and weed his garden. She wished he hadn't gone, since she was dying to speculate why the Yankee boy was living in the barn. And she hoped Johnny wouldn't say anything to Caleb. He had a bigger mouth than Johnny's friend Dan.

She remembered the muffins in the pantry, hoping they

were still there. What else could she bring him besides the
muffins? They didn't have any more juice boxes. Her mother
rarely bought them, only when they were on sale at the sal-
vage grocery store, where they could buy groceries at the
cheapest price.

But they did have an old thermos. She could clean it out
and fill it with water. She could also take a small wedge
of Swiss cheese. She'd have to cut the piece small so her
mother wouldn't realize anything was missing. That would
have to be enough. At least for now.

By the time suppertime rolled around, Johnny seemed
like himself again. He and Caleb had earned ten dollars each,
which *Daed* promptly put in the savings jar.

Mary Beth listened as everyone talked at the table, taking small bites of her food. She ate all of her sloppy joe, but
didn't finish her french fries. Fortunately, no one noticed,
and she volunteered to clean the kitchen by herself. "You
should rest, *Mami*," she said.

"*Danki*, Mary Beth." Her mother smiled. "I appreciate it."

When everyone had left the kitchen, she found another
plastic baggie and put in her leftover french fries, then added
them to the small pile of food she had stashed earlier. She
hoped he didn't mind cold fries and warm cheese.

Later that night she waited until after everyone went to
bed; then she threw the sheet off her body. She hadn't even
changed out of her dress and still had her black *kapp* on. She
took her flashlight off the nightstand and crept downstairs
to find her food stash.

But as she opened the door, she heard it creak, just as it had the night before. She held her breath, hoping once again she wouldn't be caught. When the house remained silent, she shoved the screen door open and went outside. There was still enough moonlight to light her path. She couldn't run carrying the food, but she walked briskly across the field—as it was last night, time was of the essence. But when she arrived at the barn, it was empty. Had she risked getting in trouble for nothing?

Suddenly she heard something move inside the barn. Her pulse pounding, she flicked on her flashlight and shone it at her special corner. A boy was crouched there, his head hanging down, hiding his face. He hadn't left after all. She walked toward him. But when he faced her, she gasped. "Johnny! What are you doing here?"

He looked just as surprised to see her. "What do you mean me? What are *you* doing here?"

"I asked you first."

He rose, keeping his hands behind his back. "I, um, I . . ."

"What do you have behind your back?"

"*Nix.*"

But it wasn't nothing, Mary Beth knew that. "What are you hiding?"

"I said *nix.*" He backed away but still kept his hands behind his back.

"Johnny, I can see you have something. Why won't you show it to me?"

He moved toward her, sighing. "Fine." Then he held out a small plastic bag. It was filled with an apple, a brand-new toothbrush still in its wrapper, and a piece of bread.

She had to smile at his unusual offering. "You were going to bring him that?"

"It's not much, I know, but it's something."

"I thought you didn't care about what happened to him."

"I don't. At least I didn't think I did. But you were right. We have to help him. It's our way."

Mary Beth nodded and showed him her stash.

"I wondered where the other two muffins went. I wanted those."

"We can have muffins anytime. Don't you think it's better if he has them? Especially if he has nothing but crackers to eat?"

"*Ya.*"

Mary Beth looked around. "Is he here?"

Johnny shook his head. "Nope. Haven't seen him. But he was here earlier."

"How do you know?"

He knelt down and picked up a box of crackers, shaking the box upside down. "The juice is still here, though."

She turned around, flashing the light around the barn, then crossed the room and sat down on the blanket by Johnny, putting the flashlight between them. "I wonder where he went."

"Probably back home."

"I don't think he has one."

"Of course he has one." Johnny sat down across from her. "Everyone has a home."

"Then why wouldn't he tell us his name?"

"Maybe he didn't want to. He didn't ask us our names, did he?"

"But we gave them to him anyway."

"You did, not me."

"So what if I did? Maybe if we hadn't scared him off, he would have told us who he was."

Johnny picked up a piece of hay and tucked it between his teeth. "I doubt it. He seemed pretty set on not saying much."

Mary Beth nodded. The boy's reluctance had only fueled her questions, which she spoke out loud. "Why was he wearing a sweatshirt? It's too hot for that. And what about his ripped-up jeans and how dirty he was?"

"That doesn't mean much. *Buwe* get dirty."

"Not that dirty." She looked at Johnny, part of his face lit up by the flashlight. She could tell by the way he was staring at the ground, thoughtfully chewing on the strand of hay, that he was just as troubled as she was. "Why were you acting so *seltsam* this morning?" she asked.

He frowned. "I wasn't acting weird."

"You were too. Even *Mami* and *Daed* thought you were sick." She leaned forward. "I know you were worried about him too."

He shrugged. "Maybe. A little." His gaze shot up. "But if you tell anyone, I'll deny it."

Mary Beth looked at him and grinned, glad to know her

brother did have some compassion in him. "I won't. I promise." She picked up the flashlight and rolled it around in her hand. "We should probably get back. We can't keep sneaking out at night. We're gonna get caught one of these days."

"Chicken."

Now that sounded like the Johnny she was used to. "You can call me chicken all you want," she said, standing up. She brushed the dirt off her dress. "But I won't be the one getting grounded again."

They headed toward the house, neither one of them saying anything. Suddenly her journal popped into her mind for the first time. What if he'd looked at it? Bad enough he would see her private pictures, but what if he'd read what she wrote? Her most secret thoughts were in there. She'd written pages about how her brothers bugged her, her worries about her parents, even about the crush she had on Christopher Stolzfus. Her face grew hot. "Be right back," she said, whirling around and heading back to the barn. "*Geh* on ahead, I'll catch up."

"Where are you going?"

She stopped and looked at him. "I forgot something."

"Can't you wait to get it tomorrow?"

"*Nee*," she said, starting to move again. "I don't know if I can come back tomorrow. It will only take me a second."

Johnny pulled his flashlight out of his pocket. "You sure you don't want me to wait?"

"I'm sure."

He turned and left while she went back to the barn to

get her journal. Before she entered the barn, she heard
something moving inside. Had he come back after she and
Johnny left? She immediately turned off her flashlight. If he
was in the barn, she didn't want to scare him away.

There was still enough moonlight for her to see shadows,
and she peered inside. Sure enough, there was someone
over in the corner. She heard the rustling of a plastic bag.
Quietly she stepped inside, not wanting to let him know she
was here. Just as she neared, he turned around, then jumped
to his feet.

"Wait! Don't go!"

Sawyer knew it was a bad idea to stay here. He should have
left at sundown, like he'd planned. But for some reason he
couldn't leave. Not just yet. And when he saw the kid enter
the barn a little while ago, he had to see why he'd come
back. He waited on the back side of the barn, then heard the
boy's sister join him. Sawyer couldn't tell what they were
saying, but as soon as they left, he went inside the barn.
When he saw the food there, his empty stomach rumbled.
Cheese. Muffins. Even a thermos of water. And strangely
enough, a toothbrush. He ran his tongue over his grungy
teeth. Guess they were trying to tell him something. And
although his body wanted to run, his hunger pinned him
in place.

Now for the second time he'd been caught.

She flipped on her little flashlight, but instead of pointing it directly in his face like her brother had yesterday, she held it in front and to the side. "You came back."

"Not for long." He picked up the bag of food and shoved it in his pocket, then stood up.

"Where are you going?"

"None of your business."

"Okay. Will you at least tell me your name?"

He squinted at her. "Why do you want to know?"

"I'm curious. You know my name; it's only fair I know yours."

He tilted his head to the side, and his floppy, greasy bangs slid across his forehead. He couldn't remember the last time he'd had a bath. He must stink something fierce. He took a step away from her. "Too bad. Life isn't fair."

"I know that. Look, my brother and I brought you food—"

"I didn't ask for it."

"I know you didn't, but we brought it anyway. We thought you might be hungry."

He looked away, hating that she was right. "Thanks," he managed to say, almost choking on the word. He didn't like being dependent on anyone, especially now. He needed to be able to look after himself. Somehow he didn't think he was doing such a great job of that.

The girl moved toward him, still shining the light away from his face. He took the opportunity to look at her and noticed for the first time that she wore a funny dress, like a lot of the women wore around here. She also had that funny hat on her head, only hers was black instead of white. It reminded him of pictures he'd seen in school of the pioneers. The women always had something on their heads. A bonnet, he thought it was called.

"Why do you dress like that?" he asked, unable to stop himself before the question came out.

She looked down at her clothes, then back up at him. Even though the barn was mostly dark, he could still make out the puzzled expression on her face. "I'm Amish. We all dress like this."

"Amish? Is that like a cult or something?"

Her frown deepened. "A cult? What's that?"

"You know, like witches or devil worshippers—"

He heard her gasp. *"Nee!* We're Christians! We worship God."

"Oh." He didn't have much use for God. In fact, Sawyer wasn't even sure he existed. He'd been to church a couple of times, but he didn't remember much of it, except that the bench was hard and the preacher turned red-faced whenever he shouted out, "Praise the Lord!"

"Do you belong to a cult?" she asked.

He shook his head. "I don't belong to anyone. I'm my own person. Independent."

"What about your parents?"

He crossed his arms over his chest. "What about them?"

"Aren't they wondering where you are?"

"My parents are dead."

"Oh. I'm so sorry."

He heard the sadness in her voice. "No big deal," he said, hoping he sounded less affected than he felt. He didn't think the pain of their deaths would ever go away.

"I think it's a very big deal. How did they die?"

"Are you always this nosy?"

"*Nee*, but I am curious."

"That means the same thing as nosy." His stomach growled again.

She moved closer to him. "You can go ahead and eat, you know. I also brought you some water."

"I saw that."

They both stood there for a moment, neither one of them saying anything. Why was she still here? He wished she would go home. Then he could eat the food—food she had brought, he reminded himself—and leave this place forever when he was done.

Instead of going away, she walked up next to him and sat down on the blanket. She patted the empty space beside her. "Here. Sit down. Don't worry, I'm not gonna bite you."

He thought about bolting, but his hunger and weariness overcame him. He really needed to eat, and he had no idea where his next meal would come from. "All right. But just for a minute." He yanked the bag out of his pocket and sat down. Then he ripped it open and pulled out the muffin. He offered her the other one. "Want it?"

She shook her head. "No. That's all for you."

He bit into the sweet, delicious muffin, forcing himself not to shove it down his throat in one bite.

A bark sounded right outside the barn, and the black-and-white dog trotted inside. Sawyer saw Mary Beth smile and hold out her arms. "Roscoe!"

Roscoe went straight to her, sniffed her outstretched hand, then went to the other side of Sawyer and sat down. "He's your dog?" Sawyer asked.

She shook her head. "*Nee*. He visits every once in a while. He's a *gut* dog. He seems to like you too."

Sawyer didn't feel the need to tell her that if it wasn't for the dog—Roscoe—he would have gone crazy by now. Roscoe had kept him company during the dark nights, helping Sawyer keep his fear at bay. Instead he stayed quiet and continued eating, giving small morsels to the dog.

She continued to watch him. "So if your parents died, who are you living with? And how did you get here to Middlefield?"

He polished off the muffin and reached for the cheese. He hated Swiss cheese, but right now he was so hungry it tasted like heaven. He could see she was waiting for him to answer. But he didn't want to tell her the truth. If he did, she might tell someone. Then he'd have to go back.

He'd rather die than do that.

Why won't he tell me his name?

Mary Beth didn't know what to make of the smelly, secretive boy sitting across from her. When he told her his parents were dead, she felt sad and very sorry for him. She couldn't stand the thought of anything happening to her parents. Or her brothers, even though they drove her crazy. She thought about all the times she wished she was alone, how she had escaped to this barn to spend time away from her family. But she always had them to go *back* to. This boy seemed to be truly alone. "I wish you'd tell me your name."

He didn't say anything for a while, just took another bite of the Swiss cheese. She thought she saw him make a face, but he finished off the last morsel without complaint. After the muffin and the cheese, he had to be thirsty. She took the thermos, unscrewed the cap, and poured a cup of cool water. When she handed him the drink, he said, "Sawyer."

"What?"

"My name is Sawyer. But don't ask me my last name because I'm not telling."

"That's a strange name." She motioned for Roscoe to come sit by her, but he stayed put, as if he were guarding Sawyer. Jealousy gnawed at her, but only for a second. Sawyer was alone as far as she knew. Roscoe must have known that too.

"No stranger than Mary Beth. That sounds like an old lady's name."

"It's an Amish name," she said, her pride pricked. "There are a lot of Amish girls and women who have the name Mary, and they're not old."

"So everyone who wears those weird hats and the guys with the funny haircuts—they're Amish like you?"

"I don't see what's so funny about the haircuts. They look *gut*."

"What does that mean?"

"Good. It's *Dietch*."

"*Dietch*?"

"Our language. You're not from here, are you?"

He looked away. "It doesn't matter where I'm from. It matters where I'm going."

"And where is that?"

He shrugged. "Not sure. Anywhere but here."

"But there have to be some adults who are worrying about you. What about an aunt or uncle?"

"Don't have any." He took a drink, then set the thermos top down and picked up the apple and bit into it.

She frowned. "I don't understand. How can you not have any family at all?"

"It happens. Like I said, life isn't fair." Bitterness coated his words. He took another bite of the apple, wiping away the juice that dribbled down his chin. "Are you going to be in trouble for bringing me this?"

"I might."

He looked at her. "You shouldn't have bothered."

"But you needed the food. You're obviously hungry."

"I could have gotten it from somewhere else. I've been doing just fine before I met you and what's-his-face."

"Johnny."

"Yeah, that kid. He's your brother?"

"My twin brother. I'm the oldest."

"I thought you were twins."

She frowned. "That's what I just said."

"Then how can you be the oldest?" He bit into the apple again, chomping loudly.

"I am, by four minutes. Then after me and Johnny were born, my brother Caleb came along. He's ten. I also have a younger brother named Micah, who's a year and a half. And *Mami*'s expecting another baby in January."

He tossed the apple core in the middle of the barn floor. "One big happy family," he said caustically.

She frowned and looked at the apple core. "What did you do that for? This might be a barn, but that doesn't mean you can junk it up." She jumped up from the blanket and went to pick up the apple core. One side was layered with dirt. "We are a happy family. We fight sometimes and have our fair share of worries. But we all love—"

The light in the barn suddenly went out. She spun around in time to see Sawyer disappear out the door. With her flashlight. Leaving her in the dark. "Sawyer?" She called out his name, waiting for him to come back. After a few minutes, she knew he wasn't going to. "Roscoe?" When the dog didn't appear at her side, she knew he had abandoned her too.

Angry, she made her way through the darkened barn to the outside. She looked up in the sky. A huge cloud had covered the moon, leaving her in almost complete darkness. Her palms grew damp. How could he do this to her? She'd brought him food, food that she had saved from her own plate! And how did he repay her? By stealing her flashlight and leaving her alone.

A lump formed in her throat as she walked home in the

dark, finding her way more from memory than from sight. She had thought her brothers could be jerks, but Sawyer took that prize. All her life she'd heard how important it was to help your neighbors. How God wanted everyone to treat other people like they would want to be treated. So she did what she thought was the right thing. And what had happened? She'd been left in the dark, her flashlight stolen by a kid who didn't care about anyone but himself.

Even though she'd crossed this field dozens of times, she'd never done it in complete darkness. Every little sound echoed loudly in her ears, the blades of grass tickling her legs making goose bumps break out on her skin. A dog barked in the distance, and she jumped. Maybe it was Roscoe. Her pulse slowed slightly. Then she heard a howl. That didn't sound like Roscoe at all. She knew there were coyotes around here, even though she'd never seen any. What would she do if a coyote attacked? Holding out her hands in front of her, she peered into the darkness, unable to see anything. She wouldn't even know where to run.

She suddenly felt something against her legs, and it wasn't grass. It felt soft. Like fur.

She froze, unable to move. The sound of panting filled her ears. Another howl sounded in the distance, this time closer. She felt the fur against her legs. Then something wet and cold pressed against her ankle. She wanted to scream, but the only sound that came out was a high-pitched squeak.

Then the something licked her calf. Once, twice. Glancing

down, she saw the shadow moving around. The clouds parted slightly, and she saw a glimpse of white fur. "Roscoe!"

Bending down, she put her arms around the dog, and Roscoe licked her face. Her heartbeat slowed, and she hugged him tight. "Thank goodness it's only you! You scared me to death! Worse than Johnny ever did."

Roscoe responded with another lick.

Relieved, and feeling much safer with Roscoe by her side, she stood and headed back to the house. Her anger at Sawyer had lessened a bit, but not completely. She thought about the howling she heard. If they were wolves, would Sawyer be safe? Then she remembered he had taken her flashlight. *Ya*, the little thief would be fine, she realized, frowning. As she reached the backyard, she was glad to be home.

Johnny was sitting on the back steps. When he saw her, he stood up. At least this time he didn't scare her.

"Where have you been?" he hissed, keeping his voice low. "You said you'd be right back!"

She didn't answer right away.

"Mary Beth? What took you so long? And where's your flashlight?"

"Sawyer took it."

"Who?"

"The *bu*. You know, the one we brought food for? He ate our food, then stole my flashlight when I wasn't looking." She sighed.

"You okay? He didn't hurt you, did he?" Johnny sounded upset.

"*Nee*, I'm fine." But she wasn't really. She'd been scared half out of her mind and felt foolish that she had been taken advantage of.

"Where did Roscoe come from?" Johnny bent down and started petting the dog.

"He was in the barn with us; then he disappeared. A little while later he showed up in the field and walked home with me." *Thank goodness.* She'd probably still be out there, frozen with fear, if Roscoe hadn't shown up.

Johnny rubbed Roscoe's ears, then stood up. "We're gonna get your flashlight back. Right now."

"Forget it." She waved him off. "Let him have it. I don't care anyway. He told me he was leaving and not coming back."

"But we could still catch him."

With Johnny's lightning speed she knew he could, but what would be the point? Besides, if they stayed out any longer, their parents would find out.

"No," she said tiredly. "I'm going to bed. See you in the morning." She went inside quietly and tiptoed upstairs to her room. She undressed and went to bed, telling herself to forget all about Sawyer and her stolen flashlight. If only she would listen.

Six

MARY BETH kept busy doing her chores and watching Micah all day Saturday. And even though her activities had kept her occupied, Sawyer kept creeping into her thoughts, usually when she least expected it. But every time she thought of him, she shoved the thought away again. When she started wondering about him or felt some concern, she forced herself to think about something else, like spending time with her friends after church tomorrow. She didn't need to waste any more time on Sawyer. It wasn't as if she'd ever see him again. He had left for good and had taken her flashlight with him. She didn't need to worry about that thief. She had hoped to see Roscoe, but he hadn't yet shown up. That dog was as unpredictable as the weather. While she hung laundry on the line, she thought about church. Tomorrow's service was being held at Gabriel and Moriah Millers' home. Each family in the district took turns hosting church in their house every other Sunday. By the time a year passed, nearly everyone had had the opportunity to hold church. Her own family would host church in two weeks.

Although she wouldn't admit it to anyone, Mary Beth didn't particularly like church, at least not the services. They were three hours long, and when her family had church, they spent a whole week cleaning everything until not a single speck of dirt could be found. Even the front porch was spotless. She and *Mami* also spent a lot of time baking in preparation for the fellowship after the service. Even though every family brought something to share, they would still have to prepare some food ahead of time, as no work was allowed on Sundays—not even cooking.

Still, despite the few things she didn't like about church, there was a lot she enjoyed about Sundays. Seeing her friends, for one thing. Having a delicious lunch was another. One person she didn't look forward to seeing was Christopher Stolzfus. Even though she didn't like him anymore, she still felt weird around him. Not that he even knew she existed. Other than in her journal, she had kept those thoughts to herself. She hadn't even told her best friend Katherine about it. She had only shared her feelings with the pages of her journal.

My journal! She stopped clipping a pair of Caleb's pants to the clothesline and stared across the field. Her journal was still back at the barn; she had forgotten to pick it up when she had discovered Sawyer there. She sighed. Her special place had taken on a whole new meaning over the past month. It was no longer her private sanctuary, and she didn't even want to go back there. Now it reminded her how stupid she'd been, helping out someone she didn't know. But she couldn't leave her journal behind. Even though Sawyer had left and wasn't coming back, he had managed to find the barn and stay in there. If he could find it, then surely someone else would. Plus Johnny had staked his claim on the barn as well. If he found her journal, he would read it, and she'd never live it down.

Mary Beth picked up the empty laundry basket. There wouldn't be time to sneak out and get it tonight. The family took turns taking baths on Saturday nights, and sometimes she had to help Micah with his. Besides, she was sick and tired of sneaking out of the house in the middle of the night, worrying if she was going to get caught. The journal would be safe until Sunday afternoon. When they returned from the Millers', she could run over there and get it, and no one would know. That and her blanket too. Then she would be done with the old barn. The thought of losing her secret hideout saddened her, but she had to accept that it would never be the same again.

"Why is Johnny in such a bad mood?" Katherine Yoder asked Mary Beth. The girls sat down in the soft grass a few feet away from the Millers' house. Church was over and they had just had lunch. Now the older kids were setting up the volleyball net while most of the adults mingled around both outside and inside the house. Mary Beth had enjoyed the delicious lunch, which had included cold cut sandwiches, lots of cheese and crackers, three different kinds of potato salad, pickles and pickled eggs, cherry and gooseberry pie, and velvety vanilla ice cream. She ate more than her fair share on church Sundays.

Mary Beth shrugged as she and Katherine watched Johnny leaning against the side of a white-painted tool shed. He was alone and standing still, two things that were unusual for him. Most times he could be found hanging out with other boys his age. They'd all be chasing each other around the yard or joining in a game of volleyball or baseball. But today he was picking at blades of grass, frowning.

Mary Beth knew the reason for Johnny's bad mood, but she didn't tell Katherine. She didn't need to know anything about Sawyer, or Johnny's complicated feelings about the strange boy. First off, it wasn't Katherine's business. Mary Beth didn't want to encourage Katherine's crush, since she knew Johnny didn't feel the same. They were all too young for that anyway; there would be plenty of time for courting when they turned sixteen. And second, even though Mary Beth wasn't planning on going back to the barn, Johnny probably would. She didn't know if she could trust Katherine to keep this secret.

"Maybe we should go over and talk to him," she said.

"Talk to who?"

"Johnny. Who did you think I was talking about?"

Clearing her thoughts about Sawyer, she shook her head. "I think Johnny wants to be alone."

"Then maybe *I* should go and talk to him."

Mary Beth looked at her friend, marveling at how unaware she could be sometimes. "I don't think that's a *gut* idea."

Katherine faced her, tucking her legs to the side underneath her gray dress. Her *kapp* covered only part of her red hair, and she had a smattering of freckles across the bridge of her nose. Already her cheeks were turning pink in the bright sunshine. Because she was so fair skinned, Katherine usually got sunburned every time she left the house, especially if she stayed outside for any length of time. "But he looks lonely over there."

"Johnny's never lonely. But if he is, he'll go find his friends."

"But I've never seen him like that before. So sad-looking." She stuck out her bottom lip. "And so cute."

Mary Beth's stomach turned. She liked Katherine a lot, but she didn't want to spend another afternoon listening to her go on and on about how cute Johnny was. "I'd rather not talk about Johnny. It's not like I don't get enough of him at home."

Katherine slowly pulled her gaze away from him and focused on Mary Beth. "I'm sorry. But you'd know how I feel if you liked someone the way I like Johnny."

"I guess." Mary Beth wondered if her short-lived crush on Christopher could even compare with what seemed like Katherine's obsession with Johnny. She doubted it. After all, she'd only liked Christopher for a couple of months. Katherine had been after Johnny for over a year. *Ugh*. She didn't want to dwell on that at all. "Let's *geh* get some more cookies," she said, standing up.

"Aren't you full?" Katherine joined her, looking at Johnny one more time over her shoulder.

"*Nee*. There's always room for chocolate chip cookies."

The girls left the backyard and headed for the house. Mary Beth's skin felt warm from the sun. Small beads of perspiration formed on her forehead. It was a hot summer day. She hoped Sawyer was spending it in a shady place. The barn sometimes got hot inside, especially during midday.

She sucked in a breath. Why couldn't she stop thinking about him?

"Something wrong?" Katherine asked, looking puzzled.

"*Nee*," Mary Beth said quickly. Her cheeks grew hot, and not from the sunshine. "I'm fine. Just looking forward to the taste of yummy cookies."

They walked up the stairs and entered the Millers' spacious house through the back door, which led to the kitchen. This was the second time she'd been to their house for church. Gabriel and Moriah hadn't been married long but already had a young child, Verna Anne, and a baby named Ester. More than once Mary Beth had wondered what it would be like having a sister. Katherine was the closest thing she had to one. Maybe her mother would have a girl—even though there would be nearly fourteen years between them—and she'd find out. It *had* to be better than brothers!

"Hi, Mary Beth. Katherine." Moriah Miller was standing at the kitchen sink, finishing up a load of dishes. Her sister,

Elisabeth, stood next to her, drying and putting them away. They both looked very similar, their blonde hair and blue eyes the same shade. Moriah was just a little bit taller. "How are you two doing today?"

"Fine," Katherine said. "Mary Beth wanted to know if there were any chocolate chip cookies left. She's still hungry. I thought she'd eaten enough, since she had a full plate. But I guess not."

"Katherine!" It was true, but Mary Beth didn't want anyone to think she was being greedy. She looked at the two women, embarrassed.

But Moriah didn't seem to be concerned with that. "They're on the table in the dining room. There're also a couple slices of cherry pie left, too, if you want some. The gooseberry is all gone. That's my brother Stephen's favorite."

"Everything is his favorite," Elisabeth added, putting a clean glass back into the cabinet to her left. "I'm surprised he didn't polish off the cherry pie too. He's a bottomless pit when it comes to food."

"Like Mary Beth."

Mary Beth sucked in a breath and looked at Katherine. But there was no meanness in her large blue eyes. Mary Beth doubted Katherine even knew how her comment sounded.

Both Elisabeth and Moriah chuckled. "Nothing wrong with that, especially while you're young," Moriah said.

Encouraged, Mary Beth led the way into the living room and snatched two cookies off the white platter. Katherine took one round cracker, and they both went outside.

"We haven't spent any time together since school let out, Mary Beth." Katherine polished off the cracker. "I'm sure if I asked my *mutter* I could stay the night tonight."

Mary Beth paused. If Katherine spent the night, how would she get her journal? "I don't know," she said, unsure.

"Then maybe you can spend the night at my house?"

She stifled a groan. This put her in a bigger pickle. If she was at Katherine's, there wouldn't be a way for her to get her journal.

"Please? We'd have so much fun!"

Mary Beth knew they would. It had been a long time since she'd had a sleepover with Katherine, and she was suddenly excited about the idea. What should she do? "Let me ask if you can come over tonight." Somehow she'd figure out a way to get the journal.

The girls found Mary Beth's mother visiting with several women in the front room of the Millers' house. And once they had gotten permission from Katherine's mother, it was time to go home.

The teens would gather in a couple of hours at someone else's house for a singing, where they would sing hymns and hang out. Sometimes a few of them would start courting. Katherine had said more than once that she could hardly wait to attend her first singing, and hoped Johnny would take her. Mary Beth didn't have the heart to tell her that Johnny hated singing and had said more than once that he would never go to one of "those boring, stupid things."

The Mullets—plus Katherine—all loaded up in the buggy.

It was built for a large family, with two bench seats instead of one, but it was still a tight fit. Mary Beth could only imagine how it would be squeezing in another person once the baby was born. The baby would sit on *Mami*'s lap, just like Micah was doing now; then Micah would either sit between *Mami* and *Daed* or squeeze into the backseat with her, Johnny, and Caleb. Either way, it would be crowded.

Johnny had climbed in the back first. Mary Beth had started after him, but Katherine slipped in next to Johnny and immediately started talking to him. Mary Beth sighed. She climbed in and sat down next to Katherine.

"Hey, scoot over!" Caleb jumped inside and squeezed into the last empty spot next to Mary Beth. He pushed out his elbow and nudged her in the side.

"I'm as far as I can go!" she snapped. "Stop poking me with your bony elbows."

"Mary Beth, that's enough." Her father didn't look at her as he spoke, but he didn't have to. She heard his warning loud and clear.

She scowled at Caleb, who stuck his tongue out at her, giving her one more sharp elbow to the ribs. On her other side Katherine continued talking nonstop, even though Johnny simply stared out the window of the buggy as if the scenery put him in a trance. Mary Beth knew her brother well enough to know that he was bored out of his mind with Katherine's endless chattering, but was too polite to say anything. He might be a jerk to his own sister, but he had been taught good manners; they all had. Mary Beth didn't know whom she was more aggravated with—Caleb or Katherine.

Once their father had pulled the buggy into the driveway and steered the horse to a stop in front of the barn, *Daed* and Johnny unhitched Crackerjack. Katherine lingered nearby, trying to get Johnny's attention by asking questions. Johnny ignored her, focusing on Crackerjack's harness.

Mami held Micah, who had fallen asleep in her arms, and carefully walked to the front door, with Mary Beth close behind. Suddenly *Mami* tripped on the bottom step, clinging tightly to Micah.

"Mary Beth!" she yelled when she regained her balance. "What is your flashlight doing here? I could have broken my neck! Not to mention dropping your brother."

"My flashlight? Where?"

"Right here." *Mami* pointed to the small silver flashlight with her toe. "I'm surprised at you. You normally don't leave things lying around."

That's because I didn't leave it. Mary Beth looked at the flashlight, shocked. It looked just like hers. The one Sawyer had taken. But how did it get here?

"Pick it up and put it away before someone else gets hurt."

"I will. I'm sorry. It won't happen again."

Mami's features relaxed a bit. "Please see that it doesn't." She stepped around the object and went inside the house.

Mary Beth picked up the flashlight, examining it closely. It was definitely hers: she had nicked the top of it when she'd accidentally dropped it on the asphalt road one night a few months ago. Sawyer must have brought it back. He'd said he was leaving Middlefield, and a flashlight would be a useful tool to have. So why did he take it from her if he never intended to keep it? And if he was still here, where was he now? Looking around, she wondered if he was nearby.

"Is that what I think it is?" Johnny came up behind her.

She nodded, still stunned at getting it back. "Sawyer must have been here."

"Or he dropped it somewhere and someone else brought it back."

"It doesn't have my name on it, Johnny. It looks like any other flashlight."

"Then how do you know it's yours?"

She showed him the nick at the top. "No one else would recognize it. He had to be the one to drop it off. I just don't understand why."

"Maybe he felt guilty for being a low-down thief." Johnny opened the door to go inside.

"That's not a nice thing to say!"

He turned around, irritation on his face. "May not be nice, but it's the truth. What kind of person steals a girl's flashlight and leaves her to make her way home in the dark?"

"I'm not helpless, Johnny."

"Doesn't matter. He's a thief, and I can't believe he stole from you after what we did for him. I'd be happy if I never saw his face again."

Mary Beth didn't try to defend Sawyer further. Her brother had obviously made up his mind. She glanced over her shoulder. "Where's Katherine?"

"I gave her the slip." His gaze narrowed. "Next time you invite her to stay over, warn me. I'll make sure I'm not here." He turned and went inside the house, slamming the screen door behind him.

Mary Beth gripped the flashlight and sighed. A short while ago she had the same negative thoughts about Sawyer as her brother, but now everything had changed. Whether it was out of guilt or not, Sawyer had returned her flashlight. That said a lot for him right there, because a thief wouldn't return what he'd stolen. It also proved he hadn't left Middlefield, at least not yet.

"Mary Beth! I need your help for a minute!"

She heard her mother call from inside the house. "Coming!" She tried to tamp down her excitement. Sawyer was around here somewhere, she just knew it. Maybe she would find out for sure when she went after her journal at the barn tonight. She said a little prayer that he hadn't found it. If Sawyer had read her journal, she didn't know how she could ever face him.

Sawyer pulled off his heavy sweatshirt. The air inside the barn was fairly warm, but he felt instantly cooler without the thick fabric covering his body. He wished he had a T-shirt and shorts to wear. And a new pair of shoes. The sole on his left tennis shoe had started to peel back from the rest of the sneaker, exposing the ball of his foot. His white socks had turned a grungy gray color long ago.

They had said he should feel lucky to have these clothes. *Privileged* had been their exact word, even though Sawyer knew they had been hand-me-downs that had been handed down at least once before he had received them. And two weeks of living on the run without any other clothing had taken its toll on the well-worn jeans and shirt. What he wouldn't do for a change of clothes. And a bath. More than anything he wanted a bath.

He leaned back against the hay bales, ignoring the itch of the rough hay against his skin. Roscoe, who had come into the barn with him a short while ago, sniffed his smelly sneakers, then plopped down at his feet. Sawyer had tried to leave on Saturday and had spent most of the day heading east, not sure where he was going or where he would end up. But when he'd pulled out the flashlight, guilt about taking it had stopped him cold. He'd never stolen anything in his life. He couldn't keep it, so he'd spent the rest of the night coming back to Middlefield. Then he'd been so tired he'd just come back here and collapsed. Roscoe, as usual, had shown up without warning.

Sawyer had found out where she lived after following her home in the dark Friday night. He'd stopped just short of the house. In the shadows of the darkness, he had seen her brother, could even hear them whispering as he lay low in the tall grass at the edge of their property, watching them talk as Johnny pet Roscoe. He had no idea what they were saying, and it wasn't long before they had gone back inside. Then he had stood up, staring at their home for a moment, looking at the outline of a swing set in their backyard. He noticed the barn, sturdy and well built, unlike the one he currently called home. The house was two stories, and even though there wasn't a light to be seen in any window, it still beckoned to him . . . and for a moment he wanted to go inside, if only for a little while. But he couldn't. It wasn't his home. He didn't have one.

Still, he couldn't stop imagining what it was like inside Mary Beth and Johnny's home. Their mother making supper and giving hugs before bed. Their father asking how their day went, telling them how proud he was of them. Life had been that way for him once. Not anymore.

So he'd snuck back across the field where he belonged and walked into the empty, neglected barn. He finished off the rest of the food Mary Beth and her brother had brought him. Drank the water she'd poured for him. Lay down on the blanket that belonged to her. Fiddled with the flashlight he'd stolen. And even though Roscoe had stayed by his side, he didn't sleep a wink all night.

Now it was the middle of Sunday night, and he still couldn't sleep. Darkness cloaked him, and he wished he had a flashlight or a lantern. Anything to shed a little light in the almost pitch black barn. But he didn't regret returning Mary Beth's flashlight.

What should I do now? He'd wandered around the area enough to find out that he was in a town called Middlefield, which he'd never heard of. Up until a year ago, he'd lived in Lakewood all his life. Then his parents had been killed in a car accident. He had lied to Mary Beth about not having any other relatives. He had one, all right—an uncle, currently serving fifteen to twenty-five years in prison. Sawyer quickly found out what happens to an orphan who doesn't have anyone to care for him. It wasn't long before he'd been taken by a social worker and put into a group home. He was now in the foster system, she had explained, and on a waiting list for foster parents, people who would take care of him until he was eighteen years old.

Sawyer pressed the heel of his hand against his forehead. He didn't want to think about the past. He needed to figure out what to do next. He needed to leave this place before someone other than Mary Beth and her brother found him. But why was it that every time he tried, something held him back?

Looking up, he saw a flash of light through one of the rickety slats in the barn wall. A flashlight in the distance. Roscoe barked once and jumped up, ready. Someone was coming! Sawyer hopped to his feet, grabbed his stinky sweatshirt, and ran behind the hay bales. He threw the sweatshirt over his head and willed himself not to breathe. He hoped it was just Mary Beth or her brother, but he couldn't be sure.

He peeked around one of the bales as someone walked inside the barn. Mary Beth. Roscoe went to her immediately. Sawyer breathed out a sigh of relief, then quickly ducked back when she flashed the light around the room. He heard the rustle of a plastic shopping bag and risked another look. She had set the flashlight down and was unloading things from the bag. What if she had brought food again? His stomach growled loudly.

"You can come out, Sawyer. I've got something for you to eat."

Slowly he stood, then walked toward her. The hunger in his belly overruled his brain.

She turned around and looked up at him, smiling. "Hello," she said. *"Danki* for returning my flashlight."

"Danki?"

"It means thank you." She turned around and finished emptying the bag. Then she stood up, fingering one of the strings that hung from her bonnet thingie that she wore all the time. "I brought you a few things. I thought you might need them."

"I told you I'm not staying."

She faced him. "I know. You've said that more than once. But you're still here."

He frowned. "I didn't ask you to bring me anything."

"But I wanted to." She picked up the flashlight. "Especially since you were nice enough to give this back to me. How did you know where I live?"

"It's not that hard to figure out." Guilt pressed on him again. "Um, I'm sorry I took your flashlight. I shouldn't have done that."

"Nee, you shouldn't have." Roscoe sat at her feet and tilted his head in Sawyer's direction.

If Sawyer hadn't known better, he would have thought the dog was sharing her disapproval too. "You don't have to agree with me so fast."

She smiled. "I do when you're telling the truth." She took a step toward him, and he saw her wrinkle her nose a bit, then look away, as if trying to hide her reaction. But he didn't blame her. He knew he smelled, and it embarrassed him. But he wouldn't let her know it did.

"Are those all the clothes you have?"

He hesitated for a moment, then nodded. The only other thing he'd taken from the last foster home was a dollar bill he had saved since his parents died. He still had it, although he'd been tempted to spend it on food. But his father had given it to him the day he died, and Sawyer couldn't bear to part with it. It was the only connection he had to his real family. "Nothing wrong with them."

"Other than being stained, torn, and smelly, you're right. They're perfectly fine."

"Hey, at least I don't dress in a Halloween costume. Where do you get your clothes? Little Old Ladies R Us?"

"Take that back."

Sawyer and Mary Beth both turned in the direction of Johnny's voice. Despite the dimness of the barn, Sawyer could see anger clouding Johnny's features.

"What are you doing here?" Mary Beth sounded surprised to see him.

Johnny took several steps forward, ignoring her. "You have no right to insult my sister! Take it back."

Sawyer stood up straight. "Listen, hick, I've given bigger, meaner kids than you a beat-down." And he had too. Once. In one of the foster homes. The kid had been high on drugs at the time and had passed out after the second punch. But Sawyer still counted it as a victory. "You don't scare me."

"You don't scare me, either."

The boys stared each other down, waiting to see who would make the first move.

Seven

"Stop it!" Mary Beth inserted herself between Johnny and Sawyer as Roscoe barked and danced around the boys. "You're both acting stupid."

Johnny spoke in *Dietsch*. "He's being a jerk, Mary Beth."

"Speak English!" Sawyer demanded. He looked at Mary Beth. "What did he just call me?"

Mary Beth's eyes darted from one boy to the other, both of them so angry she could practically feel it like heat. She'd been the one to start this mess, and it was up to her to clean it up. She hoped she could straighten them both out before they came to blows. She ignored Sawyer's question, not wanting to pour gasoline on the fire. "Johnny, I'm the one who owes him an apology."

"You do?" he and Johnny said in unison.

"*Ya.*" She turned to Sawyer. "I didn't mean to insult your clothes. What I said didn't come out right." She lifted up the folded shirt and pants she'd brought from home. "I thought you could wear these so I could wash and fix the ones you have on now."

"What?" Sawyer's eyes grew wide with disbelief. "Are those Amish?"

"*Ya,*" she said.

"And they're mine." Johnny came over to her and reached out for his shirt, but she jumped back, holding the garments behind her back. "You have no right to give him my clothes," he said.

"*Old* clothes," Mary Beth pointed out. "I found some of your old pants and a shirt you haven't worn in a long time."

"You went through my clothes?" Johnny fumed. "Without asking me?"

She bit her bottom lip. At the time, finding clean clothes for Sawyer had seemed like a good idea. Now she wasn't so sure. "I didn't think you'd mind. What are you doing out here, anyway?"

"I heard you leave."

She gasped. "You heard me?" Had her parents woken up?

"Don't worry, no one else heard. But you really need to practice sneaking out."

"I could give you a few pointers," Sawyer said.

They both looked at him. Mary Beth was surprised at his lighthearted tone. He even had a half grin on his face, as if watching them bicker was amusing. Shrugging, he added, "I've had plenty of practice."

"We do fine on our own," Johnny said. Clearly he wasn't as quick to simmer down.

"I can see that." Sawyer took a step closer to Mary Beth. "Did I hear you right? You're offering to wash my clothes?"

She nodded. "I don't see how I can sneak you in the house for a bath, though."

A couple of inches taller than she was, he peered down at her. "Are you saying I stink?"

Roscoe sat down by Sawyer's feet. The dog sniffed his shoes, then barked.

There she went again, opening her mouth and saying the wrong thing. "Um, no?" she said. Then she saw him smile.

"Yeah, right. I can barely stand the smell myself. Roscoe thinks so too." He reached around and took the clothes from her, suddenly looking sheepish. "I, uh . . . um, thanks."

Mary Beth smiled too. He was puzzling, that's for sure. One minute he was stealing the flashlight from her; the next minute he was giving it back. He could turn angry in a moment and become calm the next. He was filled with secrets, yet she could see his emotions clearly. He was scared. Tired. Lonely. And trying desperately to hide all that from everyone.

"Shouldn't I have a say in this?" Johnny piped up, sounding less upset than before. "Those are my clothes, after all."

Mary Beth and Sawyer both looked at him. "Letting him use them is the right thing to do," Mary Beth said.

"*Nee*. The right thing would be to tell *Mami* and *Daed* about him."

Sawyer thrust the clothes at Johnny. "Forget it. I'm outta here."

"Wait," Mary Beth said. She looked at her brother. "Why did you say that?"

"Because it's true," he said, speaking in *Dietsch* again. "He's a runaway, and I don't trust him. He's already stolen from you—"

"And gave it back," she pointed out.

"How do you know he's not planning to break into our house and steal our stuff?"

"What do we have to steal that's worth anything, Johnny? Other than food?"

"The savings jar, remember?"

"Hey, I'm standing right here," Sawyer interrupted. "I know you're talking about me, so you might as well say it in English." He looked from Mary Beth to Johnny. "Never mind." He started toward the door, but Mary Beth ran around and blocked his way.

"Don't go. Not yet."

"Why does it even matter to you?" Sawyer looked her straight in the eye. "Why do you care? No one else does."

"I don't believe that."

"Oh, believe it. Do you know how lucky you are?" He glanced at Johnny over his shoulder. "Both of you. You have a nice house. Parents who care about you. Good clothes, even if they are weird-looking. Enough food to eat. Me? I've got nothing but these stinky clothes."

"What happened to your parents?" Johnny asked.

"They died," Mary Beth said in an embarrassed whisper. "Remember? I told you that."

Johnny moved closer to Sawyer, his expression a little sheepish. "Sorry. I forgot. Where did you go after your parents died?"

"Foster care. You know what that is?"

Mary Beth and Johnny both shook their heads.

"You don't want to know."

"*Ya*, I do," Mary Beth said.

"It's where kids go when they don't have parents. Either their parents died or they can't take care of them. You go live with foster parents. They're strangers. You have to live in their house and follow their rules. No matter what." He glanced away.

"I can't imagine it's worse than living out here alone," Mary Beth said.

"Trust me, it is." His face scrunched up into a scowl. "I'm not going back there. And that's what's gonna happen if you tell someone about me. The police will pick me up and put me right back in the system."

"System?" Johnny asked.

"The foster care system. First I'll be in the group home. Boy, is that a lot of fun." With each word Sawyer's voice grew more bitter. "No privacy. Kids picking on you all the time. Nothing is your own. But that's a picnic compared to being with a foster family, especially one that only cares about the check they get for taking you in. Or thinks it's okay to whip you with a belt on your palm whenever they've had too many beers."

Mary Beth cringed at Sawyer's words. She didn't understand

about the family getting a check, but getting whipped was another story. Her palms tingled just hearing about it. Now she understood why he'd run away.

"You're making that up," Johnny said.

Sawyer shrugged. "I don't care if you believe me or not."

"So you're just going to live here forever? What about winter? How will you keep warm?"

"By then I'll have everything figured out."

Mary Beth wondered if he knew how ridiculous and desperate he sounded. She didn't think so. Yet she didn't want to scare him away. At least while he was here she could help him out. "We're not going to say anything, are we, Johnny. Right?" When Johnny didn't answer she repeated, *"Right?"*

Johnny sniffed. The old hay in the barn must have kicked up his allergies. "All right, fine. I won't say anything. At least not yet."

Sawyer let out a long breath.

"But if you're gonna stay here, you gotta get a bath." Johnny held his nose. "Seriously. Our pigpen's starting to smell better than you."

Mary Beth frowned. "Just how's he supposed to do that? You know we can't sneak him in the house."

Johnny snapped his fingers and looked at Sawyer. "The pond. We've got one on our back property. No one goes back there, especially at night. We used to have a few fish in it, but I haven't seen any in a long time, so you don't have to worry about anyone fishing it."

"I can bring you some soap," Mary Beth said, liking the idea.

Sawyer nodded. "That sounds good. What about my clothes?"

She tapped her finger on her chin for a moment, thinking. "I'll try to bring the soap to you sometime tomorrow. Then when you're done you can leave your clothes and I'll pick them up."

"I think it would be easier if we had a pick-up spot closer to our house," Johnny said. "We can't keep coming out here at night."

"What about right by the pond?" Mary Beth suggested. "We can put things in one of those wood crates *Daed* has in the shed."

"You can pick things up there," Johnny added, looking at Sawyer. He brushed the back of his hand underneath his nose and sniffed again.

Mary Beth agreed. "You can also drop things off, like your clothes."

Sawyer didn't say anything for a long time. She thought for a minute he might tell them no. "All right," he finally said. "The pond it is."

Mary Beth grinned as she glanced at Sawyer. He looked at her for a moment, and she could see the relief in his brown eyes. She was glad he had finally accepted their help.

Mary Beth had brought other things—a plastic comb she'd found in one of the bathroom drawers, the extra peanut butter sandwich she'd made earlier at lunch, and a wooden yo-yo she'd had since she was little. The yo-yo was a last-minute idea. He had to be bored staying out here all alone. She had also decided to leave him her flashlight. She now knew she could make it home in the dark without a problem, especially if Roscoe came with her. She glanced around, looking for him. He wasn't in the barn. "Anyone seen Roscoe?"

"He was just here." Sawyer glanced around, too, while Johnny went to look out the front door of the barn. He popped back in and shook his head.

"He must have left while we were talking."

Mary Beth shrugged and looked at Johnny. He didn't have to say anything; his expression told her they needed to stop wondering about the dog and get going. "Have a *gut* night," she said to Sawyer as she and her brother started to leave. She handed him her flashlight. Johnny had already walked outside when Sawyer called her name.

"Mary Beth. Wait."

Turning around, she faced him.

He looked down at the ground, then back up at her, holding the flashlight at an angle so they could both clearly see each other's faces. "Why are you and Johnny doing this? Why bother?"

"Because you need us to."

He didn't say anything for a long moment, just stared at the ground. Then he looked at her. "I don't have anything to give back."

"We don't want anything." She smiled. "God calls us to help our neighbor. All Amish do that. Right now you're our neighbor, and you're in trouble. I'm just glad we can give you a hand." With that she turned around and started to leave, then remembered one of the reasons she'd come. She hurried past Sawyer and felt underneath her blanket for her journal. Tucking it under her arm, she ran past him and out the door, rushing to catch up with Johnny.

Sawyer looked down at the flashlight in his grimy hand, still trying to understand what Mary Beth had just said. She thought God wanted them to help him out?

"Yeah, right," he said out loud. Like God cared anything about Sawyer Thompson. If he did, Sawyer wouldn't need Mary Beth and Johnny's help. He'd be at home with his family. Happy. The way things used to be before everything fell apart. Back then he had friends. Made good grades. Planned to play on the high school football team. All that disappeared in one night. Everything he'd known and loved had vanished when a drunk driver slammed head-on into his parents' car.

Now there would be no football team and no worrying about his grades. He didn't have friends anymore; he'd lost touch with them when he'd been put in foster care. His life consisted solely of living from day to day, and even that would be a problem once summer ended. Johnny was right. Winters were cold in Ohio. He couldn't stay here past early September.

What would he do after that? He had no idea, and it scared him.

He forced the thoughts away, focusing on right now.

Forgetting the past and ignoring the future—that was the only way he knew how to cope. Thanks to Mary Beth and Johnny—mostly Mary Beth—he had what he needed to get through tonight and tomorrow. He still couldn't believe they were being so generous. When Johnny had started yammering about telling their parents, fear had gripped him . . . but instead they had decided to help him. He still didn't know for sure if they would say anything, but he had to trust that they wouldn't.

Trust. He hated the word. He'd trusted his social worker, Mrs. Prescott. He'd trusted his foster parents. Both had been mistakes—ones he didn't plan on repeating again.

He had to face it: he was at the mercy of these Amish kids. And until he figured out another plan, he'd have to accept that. But only until he could come up with something else. Because despite their help, he was alone. No one cared about him, especially not God.

He lay down on the blanket and closed his eyes. A few minutes later he heard Roscoe come inside the barn. The dog sniffed his feet, then lay against Sawyer's side. Sawyer couldn't help but smile a little. At least Roscoe cared enough to come back.

With quiet steps Mary Beth followed her brother inside the house and back up the stairs to their bedrooms. Johnny went into his bedroom, and she continued to creep down the hallway, praying she wouldn't wake anybody up. She entered her bedroom and glanced at Katherine's sleeping form on the bed. Mary Beth had given Katherine her bed and made a pallet on the floor out of a couple of old quilts. Just as her head touched the pillow, Katherine spoke.

"Where *were* you?" she whispered.

Mary Beth froze, gripping the edge of the quilt. *Oh no!* "What do you mean?"

Katherine turned on the small battery-powered lamp sitting on the nightstand next to Mary Beth's bed. She squinted at the bright light, then opened her eyes wider as they adjusted. "I woke up to go to the bathroom a little while ago, and you weren't here. I thought maybe you were fixing a snack in the kitchen, but I didn't see you there, either. And you weren't in the bathroom because I had just finished using it." Katherine sighed, as if figuring all that out had hurt her brain. "So where were you?"

Mary Beth's palms grew damp. She couldn't tell Katherine she'd snuck out of the house. What if Katherine told? And if she didn't, she'd bombard Mary Beth with questions, questions she couldn't answer, even if she wanted to.

She heard Katherine shifting in the bed. "Mary Beth? Why aren't you answering me?"

Mary Beth rolled onto her side and faced Katherine, who was now sitting up. Her mind whirred as she tried to think of a decent story Katherine would believe. "I went outside."

"Outside? Why?"

"To, um, count the stars," she said quickly, remembering the reason Johnny had given her when he snuck out of the house in the middle of the night. She'd believed her brother when he told her that, and maybe Katherine would believe her now. "I couldn't sleep, so I decided to count those instead of sheep."

She held her breath, waiting for Katherine's response. Mary Beth's stomach churned as her friend continued to remain silent.

Finally she spoke. "You know, I never thought of counting stars to get sleepy. I should try that sometime. I'll have to ask my parents, though. I'd get in awful trouble if I got caught sneaking out. You're lucky your parents don't mind you going outside so late at night."

They would if they knew what I was really up to. Mary Beth flopped back on her pallet, exhaling in one long breath. "*Ya.* I'm really lucky. Turn out the light, will you?"

Katherine clicked off the lamp. The springs squeaked softly as she settled back on the bed. "Does Johnny go out and count stars?" she asked in a dreamy voice.

Oh brother. I really don't want to talk about him right now. "I don't know. You'll have to ask him."

"Ooh, I will. First thing in the morning. I'll get up early and catch him before breakfast."

Mary Beth cringed. If Johnny wasn't crabby when he woke up tomorrow, he sure would be by the time Katherine finished with him. She rolled over onto her back and pulled a sheet over her weary body. As her eyelids grew heavy, her thoughts about Katherine and Johnny disappeared, replaced by Sawyer's image and memories of seeing him in the barn. She was glad he had decided to stay, even if it was for a short time.

Three days later Mary Beth and her mother were in the kitchen, cleaning up from the morning meal. They'd had pancakes for breakfast, and *Mami* was putting the syrup back in the pantry. Mary Beth heard her let out an exasperated sigh.

"Honestly, I think Johnny's eating us out of house and home." *Mami* stepped back from the pantry and held up a jar of peanut butter. "I just bought this the other day, and now it's half gone."

Mary Beth glanced over her shoulder, then turned back around and scrubbed the frying pan, keeping her gaze on the sink of soapy water in front of her. She knew if she met her mother's face, she'd look as guilty as she felt. Johnny hadn't taken more than his fair share of the peanut butter, of course. She had been fixing one extra peanut butter sandwich for Sawyer for the past few days.

"The bread is disappearing too." *Mami* set the jar on the counter and put her hands on her hips. "He must sneak in here to get a midnight snack. I'm going to give him a talking to. We can't afford for him to be eating like this. If he's that hungry, he needs to eat more at suppertime."

Mary Beth scrubbed the pot until she thought she'd rub right through the metal. She wasn't worried about *Mami* talking to Johnny about the missing peanut butter and bread. They had both agreed not to say anything about Sawyer. But what if she started noticing other things were missing? Like the bar of soap she put in the drop-off box a few days ago? Or the can of pork and beans she took to him yesterday? She had opened the top with a can opener before putting it in the box, hoping he would come before the bugs got into it. She hadn't actually seen him since they had agreed on dropping things off at the pond, but each evening when she went to check the box, it was empty, except for the other day when he had left his clothes for her to wash.

"Caleb might be guilty too," *Mami* said as she put the peanut butter back in the pantry. "He's been growing like a weed this summer."

Mary Beth rinsed off the pot and set it in the dish drainer to dry, but didn't say anything.

"Oh well. I suppose that's to be expected with boys." *Mami* moved to stand by Mary Beth. "Did you remember I have a doctor's appointment later today?"

"*Ya,*" she said, rinsing off the last dish from breakfast and putting it in the drainer. She reached inside the soapy water and pulled out the stopper.

"I'll need you to watch Micah for me. I don't want to take the boys this time."

Mary Beth hid her disappointment at the prospect of spending another afternoon babysitting her brothers. Then Sawyer popped into her thoughts, reminding her she didn't have anything to complain about. At least she had a family, even if certain members of that family were annoying sometimes.

"I asked Johnny to keep an eye on Caleb." *Mami* gave her a half smile. "But you know how that goes. Make sure you watch out for both of them. I don't want any trouble while I'm gone."

"I will." She understood her mother's reluctance to let Johnny be in charge of their younger siblings. He hadn't been the most responsible child in the family in the past. But since they'd discovered Sawyer, she'd noticed a change in Johnny. He had become a little more serious and had also been true to his word about not telling anyone about Sawyer. Right now he and Caleb were outside taking care of the yard; Johnny was using the gas-powered weed whacker to attack the tall weeds and grass that had grown against the sides of the house and barn, while Caleb cut the lawn with their old push mower.

"What time are you leaving?" Mary Beth asked her mother.

Mami glanced at the clock above the sink. "In about an hour. Mrs. Prine is coming to pick me up; then after my appointment she's taking me over to Sarah's for coffee."

"Cousin Sarah?"

"*Ya.*" She sighed, smoothing her light green dress. "I haven't seen Sarah for a while, so I'm looking forward to it. I'll be gone most of the afternoon, so would you mind starting supper for me? We've got everything we need for tuna casserole."

"Sure."

"*Danki, dochder.*" She bent down and kissed Mary Beth's

forehead. "I thought tonight would be a *gut* night for me to start teaching you how to make coats."

Mary Beth smiled. Finally she was going to learn how to do something other than sewing hems and repairing rips in clothing. "Really?"

Her mother touched Mary Beth's cheek. "Really. I know you've been wanting to learn. Lately I've asked you to do so many things you don't enjoy, especially looking after your brothers. I know Caleb can be a handful. So I think it's time you get to do something you like."

Mary Beth watched her mother leave the kitchen, and she smiled. She hoped the afternoon would go by quickly. It should, since Micah would probably take a nap around noon, and as long as Johnny kept Caleb in line, she could finish doing her other chores and maybe even have time to draw in her journal.

An hour later Mrs. Prine drove up and her mother left for the rest of the day. It was near eleven, and Mary Beth was in the middle of making lunch when Caleb burst through the door.

"Melvin wants to know if I can come over today."

She looked at her younger brother, his worn brown shoes covered in cut blades of grass, which were landing in a trail across the kitchen floor. "Caleb, your shoes! You know *Mami* would have a fit if she saw all that grass in here."

Caleb scowled and slipped off his shoes. "There. Happy?"

"Put them by the back door. Then I'll be happy."

Muttering something about bossy girls, Caleb did as he

was told, then walked over to Mary Beth. Micah was seated at the table already, pushing a small wooden train back and forth across the polished wood. "So can I *geh* to Melvin's?"

She didn't reply right away. Melvin Fisher lived a few houses down, past the abandoned barn, and well within walking distance. "I don't know. *Mami* didn't say anything about you going to your friend's house."

"C'mon, Mary Beth. Please? I'll be back before *Mami* comes home. She doesn't even have to know I'm gone." He shifted from one foot to the other, impatient. "Melvin and David are outside waiting on me. I need to let them know."

"Where's Johnny?"

"Haven't seen him."

Mary Beth groaned, setting down the knife she was using to cut up a brick of cheddar cheese. So much for Johnny becoming more serious and responsible. At least at the Fishers' she knew Melvin's mother would be watching the boys. "All right. But watch out for cars on the way down there."

He rolled his eyes. "I always do. I'm taking the scooter, 'kay?"

Caleb dashed out the door, forgetting not only his shoes, but his manners. Mary Beth thought about calling him back but changed her mind. He was fine going around barefoot. That was one of the fun things about summer—feeling the fresh grass between your toes, pressing your feet down into the cool dirt on a hot day, like today. Tomorrow was July first, and they hadn't had any rain for over a week. A glance out the kitchen window at the cloudless sky showed her it would be another dry, hot day.

She finished cutting, then placed a slice of homemade bread and butter on a plate, along with a couple of cheese slices and four apple wedges. She filled Micah's sippy cup with milk, then fed him his lunch. Johnny, whenever he decided to come home, could fend for himself.

Just as she sat down with her lunch, Johnny came into the kitchen. But he wasn't alone. She nearly dropped her plate when she saw Sawyer slowly enter the room behind him. "What are you doing here?"

Johnny pointed his thumb at her and spoke to Sawyer over his shoulder. "If I had said that, she would have gotten after me for bad manners." He looked at Mary Beth. "We have a guest for lunch and this is how you treat him?"

She gaped at both of them, then turned her focus to Johnny. "Where have you been? You were supposed to be watching Caleb."

"I was. But then I saw this one sneaking around the backyard."

Sawyer stepped out from behind Johnny. He was still wearing Johnny's old clothes, and he smelled much better. The pants were baggy around the waist and a little short at the ankles. Except for his long, shaggy hair, which was a lighter shade of brown now that it was clean, Sawyer could easily blend in with the rest of the boys in their Amish community. "I wasn't sneaking."

"Spying, then," Johnny countered.

"It gets boring in that barn all the time." He glanced down at the ground. "I was just checking things out in the area."

"Right next to our house." Johnny grinned at him. "Like I said, it's fine. *Mami's* gone for the day, so you can hang out here."

"I don't know if that's a *gut* idea," Mary Beth said, putting down her plate.

Sawyer's eyes narrowed. "Why? Afraid I'll steal something else?"

"Of course not. That's the dumbest thing I've ever heard." She gave Sawyer an exasperated look. Why was he always so negative? "But if *Mami* comes back early and you're here . . . You're the one who wanted us to keep your secret."

"And we will." Johnny walked into the kitchen. "When I saw Caleb leave with Melvin and David, I invited Sawyer to come in. *Mami* won't be back early, so we don't have to worry about that." He moved over by the counter, where the cheese lay on a carving board next to a few apples. "Is this all we have?"

"It's all I fixed for me and Micah."

"It's not gonna be enough for me and Sawyer. I'm starving." He looked at Sawyer, who was still standing by the door. "How about you?"

"I could eat."

"So that wasn't your stomach growling a minute ago?"

"Okay, fine. I'm hungry."

Micah threw his wooden toy train on the ground and

started to cry. Mary Beth went to him and gave him back the train, which he tossed on the floor again.

"I think he's done with that," Johnny said, leaning against the countertop.

Mary Beth gave her brother an annoyed look and picked up Micah from his chair. But instead of snuggling against her like he normally did, he arched his back and tried to squirm out of her grasp. When she set him down on the floor, he toddled over to Johnny, holding up his arms.

"Looks like he wants you," she said, a bit surprised. This wasn't the first time Micah had gone to Johnny, but he mostly preferred their mother or Mary Beth. Johnny picked him up. Micah leaned his chubby cheek against his shoulder.

"I'm gonna take him upstairs." Johnny headed toward the kitchen exit, then stopped. "Help Sawyer find something to eat other than that rabbit food."

He walked out of the room, leaving Sawyer and Mary Beth alone.

She turned around. Sawyer hadn't budged an inch from the door. His back was against the screen door, as if he were ready to bolt outside at any minute. Frowning, she walked toward him. She hadn't meant to make him feel bad or unwanted.

"I can go . . ." He shrank away from her as she neared. "I probably shouldn't be here anyway. I don't want you to get in trouble on account of me."

Unable to stop herself from smiling at his concern, she said, "*Nee*, it's fine. I was just surprised to see you here, that's all. Come in and sit down." She gestured at the kitchen table. "I'll find you and Johnny something to eat."

"I like cheese."

She shook her head. "Johnny's right; I'm sure we have something better."

Sawyer sat down at the table, his gaze darting around the room. "You don't have to go to the trouble."

"It's no trouble. I'll run downstairs for a minute and see what we have."

Moments later she appeared with some leftover pot roast and a small container of potato salad she'd found in one of the coolers, plus home-canned green beans. "It won't take me long to heat up the roast," she said, moving to the stove.

"Roast?"

"We had some the other night. We don't have it very often. Usually we have potatoes and carrots with it, but those are gone. That's why I brought up the potato salad." When she finished talking, she heard a loud growling noise coming from Sawyer's stomach.

He looked down at the table, his shaggy hair hiding his face. He lifted his head, brushing his long bangs back from his forehead. "Sorry."

She chuckled. "That's okay. I'll hurry up."

Eight

SAWYER'S STOMACH churned with hunger as he breathed in the delicious aroma of the pot roast Mary Beth was heating on the stove. His mouth watered so much it took everything he had not to jump up out of his seat and grab the food out of her hands. He couldn't remember the last time he'd had pot roast. Or potato salad. Or even green beans. His last foster family's idea of gourmet eating had been canned spaghetti and a pack of fruit snacks to round out the meal. Although that wasn't the case when they had a social worker visit. Then he'd gotten meat loaf, which hadn't been too bad. But once the social worker left, it was back to ramen noodles and peanut butter.

He watched Mary Beth work. She seemed to be at home in the kitchen and heated up the meal with ease. His cooking skills were limited to opening a can or a jar, putting a plate in the microwave, and pushing start.

Come to think of it, where is the microwave? He looked

around the spotless kitchen, noticing for the first time that there wasn't a microwave in sight. Or a toaster. Or a coffeemaker. None of the things his parents had kept in their kitchen. The counters were empty except for the food Mary Beth was making. He also noticed there wasn't a light on in the kitchen. When he looked up at the ceiling, he didn't see one.

Weird.

"Here you go." Mary Beth put a plate in front of him. The steam from the pot roast and green beans filled his nostrils. He'd never smelled anything so good. She then set down a glass of cold milk. But he didn't dive into the food right away. "What about Johnny? Is there enough for him?"

"*Ya.* I saved him plenty. And he can get food anytime." She sat across from him, her apple and cheese plate in front of her.

He picked up his fork. "Aren't you having any?"

"I'm fine with this. I'm not that hungry anyway."

He picked up a forkful of potato salad and moved it toward his mouth, stopping halfway when he saw Mary Beth with her head bowed and eyes closed. She was praying. He waited for her to finish, more out of politeness than respect for her prayer, then shoved the salad in his mouth. The flavors exploded in his mouth. *Awesome.*

Johnny came downstairs, looking irritated. "Micah's a stubborn kid. He didn't want to go to sleep, but I knew he was tired." He looked at Sawyer's plate, then at Mary Beth. "Where's mine?"

Mary Beth picked up an apple slice. "Over there. It's still warm."

"Why didn't you fix me a plate?"

"I didn't know when you'd be back. You're capable of dishing out your own food. Don't be such a *boppli*."

He gave her a smirk, then pulled out a plate from the cabinet and started slapping food on it. He plopped the plate on the table, and then, just like his sister had, he dipped his head and closed his eyes. A minute later he opened them and started eating.

Sawyer was too busy finishing his food to say anything, and he had all of it eaten before Mary Beth had polished off her apple slices. He drained the glass of milk and leaned back in the chair.

"How was it?" she asked.

"Delicious. Best meal I've had in forever." At least since his parents had died. His mother had been a good cook. His favorite meal had been her spaghetti and meatballs. From scratch, not a can.

"Nice change from peanut butter, I bet." Johnny shoved a slice of buttered bread in his mouth.

"I like peanut butter." He wasn't about to complain about anything these two had done for him. He didn't like to think about it, but he didn't know what would have happened to him if they hadn't been so generous. But he didn't like feeling obligated. "I'll pay you back someday. Promise."

"Don't worry about it." Johnny waved his hand. "No big deal."

But it was a big deal to Sawyer. He vowed to himself to make good on that promise. He had no idea how he would, but he'd make sure he paid back everything he owed both of them.

Johnny ate the last bite of green beans and pushed away from the table. "I promised *Daed* I would clean out the chicken coop today." He looked at Sawyer. "Wanna help?"

Sawyer had never been near a chicken, much less cleaned out a coop. Still, it sounded better than spending another afternoon alone with nothing to do. "Sure," he said, glad to be able to offer something, even if it meant shoving out chicken dung.

"Great. Meet me outside in a few minutes, then. I have to put away the lawn mower—Caleb left it out. Again. I should probably let him get in trouble for it, but then *Daed* would probably get on me too."

"Are your parents that mean?"

"Nah. They just like things done right. Plus replacing the lawn mower costs money. It's not like we have a lot to go around."

Hearing that just piled on the guilt. Seemed no matter where he was, he was a burden to someone.

After Johnny left, Sawyer stood up and carried his plate to the sink, a habit he'd had since he was little.

Mary Beth came up behind him with her plate and Johnny's. "*Danki.*"

"That means thanks, right?"

"*Ya.*"

He stepped to the side to let her put her dishes in the sink, then asked her the question that had been bugging him since he'd walked into the kitchen. "Where's the microwave?"

"We don't have one."

"Really? I thought everyone had one."

"We don't. You have to have electricity to run one."

That news shocked him. "You don't have electricity?"

"*Nee.*" She ran some water in the sink, then turned off the tap. "Never."

Wow, they really are old-fashioned. Chickens, old-looking clothes, no electricity. And then there were the horses and the funny-looking buggy things he saw every once in a while when he ventured near the road. "Why not?"

"Amish aren't allowed to use electricity in their homes."

His brows furrowed. "That doesn't make any sense. How do you see in the dark without lights?"

She looked at him, appearing more amused than annoyed by his questions. "We use gas- and battery-powered lamps and flashlights."

"Let me guess—you don't have a phone either." He knew that phones had to be plugged into an outlet in order to work. Even cell phones had to be charged on an electric charger.

"Nope. We could have a cell phone if we wanted to, as long as we kept it out in the barn."

"In the barn?" This was sounding weirder by the moment. *Who keeps a phone in the barn?*

"*Ya.*" She squirted some green dish detergent in the sink

and ran the water. "But *Daed* says they're too expensive and unnecessary."

"Then how do you call your friends? Or use the computer?"

"We don't have a computer. And we don't need to call our friends. We see them at church on Sundays, and when we're in school, and when we get together for gatherings and stuff. If we have to call someone because of an emergency, our Yankee neighbors two houses down don't mind letting us borrow their phone. But we've only had to do that a few times, mostly when scheduling doctor appointments or trying to get taxi rides."

Sawyer was dumbfounded. He couldn't imagine actually choosing not to have a computer or phone. Or electricity, for that matter. The one thing he missed most of all, except for his parents, was a computer. He missed playing online games with his friends, surfing the Web, and using instant messaging. He'd even had a cool cell phone before his parents died. But it had been taken away when he went into foster care, and his foster parents had never offered to get him one. "So your dad won't let you have electricity or a phone or a computer?" Johnny had said their dad wasn't mean, but he sure sounded like he was. Sawyer had envisioned Johnny and Mary Beth having the perfect parents. Instead they seemed really strict.

"Not having electricity isn't up to *Daed*. It's the rules of the church."

"Those rules are way harsh. I don't get why you all would stay with a church that won't let you have basic necessities."

She laughed, shutting off the water. Picking up a rag, she started wiping the dishes. "We have all the basic necessities and more. Computers and phones aren't necessities. We get along just fine without them."

"So it doesn't bother you that the church won't let you have these things?"

"Not at all. We don't have cars, either, but we get from one place to another in our buggies. And if we need to go far away, like *Mami* did for her appointment, then we make arrangements for a taxi. Even if I could have a car, I wouldn't. They're noisy and smell funny."

"Have you ever ridden in one?"

"A few times. Most of the time I walk or ride with *Daed* in the buggy." She turned on the tap again and rinsed the soapy plates, then set them in a plastic drainer in the other side of the double sink.

Sawyer was fascinated. "Those things don't move very fast."

"They don't need to. If you ask me, Yankees move too fast. Always rushing around in their cars, talking on their phones, doing that texting thing." She mimicked pushing the buttons on a phone with her thumbs, soap bubbles flying in the air.

"How do you know about texting?"

"I don't live in a cave," she said, looking at him. Grabbing the rag, she squeezed it out and slid it across the edge of the sink, catching up the excess water. "I've been to the grocery store. And shopping at Walmart. I've seen people walking around with phones, pushing all those buttons." She shook her head. "That's not for me."

"So let me get this straight. The Amish live without electricity, phones, or computers."

"*Ya.* Except if they need them where they work. Then they're allowed to use them. But in the home, it's forbidden."

"Because of the rules of the church."

"Exactly."

"Why do they have those rules?"

She hesitated a bit before speaking. Then she looked up at him, her blue eyes meeting his. "I'm not sure exactly why, other than all that stuff is a bad influence. It brings in the outside world. Makes us tempted to do things we shouldn't do, like spendimg all our time in front of the TV instead of doing our chores or visiting with our friends. I'll find out more about it when I join the church."

"You're not even a member of the church?"

"Not yet."

He scratched his head. This was making less and less sense to him.

"When I turn sixteen, I can make that decision. Or if I want to wait, I can. I can even decide not to join if I don't want to. But once I do, I have to follow all the rules, like I do now. And I have to make sure my family follows them."

Now instead of fascinating, it was confusing. "Seems like an awful lot of trouble to me."

Her eyes grew wide. "Trouble?"

"Electricity, cell phones, cars—all that stuff is supposed to make your life easier. Why would you choose not to use them? It only makes your life harder."

"Life is hard anyway. Do you really think your life was easier because you had all those things?"

He thought about her question. Did a computer keep his parents from dying? Did a cell phone save him from abusive foster parents? "That's different. My parents are dead. I'm alone. That's why my life is hard."

Compassion filled her eyes. "I'm sorry."

Turning away, he said, "Doesn't matter."

"It does." She stopped wiping the counter and stared at him. "You're not alone, you know. God is always with you."

"Whatever. Trust me, God doesn't care what happens to me."

"Don't say that!" She looked genuinely surprised. And a bit offended. "He does care about you. He cares about everyone."

"How do you know?"

"It's in the Bible, for one thing. I've heard my parents say it too."

"I don't believe in the Bible. And parents can be wrong."

"Sawyer?" Johnny poked his head inside the back door. "Are you coming or what?"

"Be right there," he said over his shoulder. He looked back at Mary Beth. "Thanks for lunch. And for the clothes."

But she didn't reply. She only looked at him with sadness.

Mary Beth watched the door shut after Sawyer left to join Johnny in the chicken coop. She stared at the empty kitchen, her mind filled with thoughts about their conversation. She had welcomed Sawyer's questions about the Amish. He seemed genuinely interested—and not because he wanted to make fun of the way she dressed or how she was different from him. She'd heard the snickers and noticed the stares of other people, not always kids, whenever she and her family went to a Yankee place like Walmart. Sawyer, at least, seemed to want to know more about the way she and her family lived, and also why they lived that way. That part of the conversation didn't trouble her.

Hearing what he said about God and the Bible did.

She'd never known anyone who didn't believe in God. She also couldn't understand why he didn't. It made her sad to think he thought he was truly all alone. Even though he had run away from home, God had been with him all along. She believed that. But she didn't know how she'd be able to convince him of it.

After she dried the dishes and put them away, she tiptoed upstairs to check on a still-sleeping Micah; then she went outside to tend the garden. Caleb and *Daed* had made a scarecrow last week, and they'd hung up foil pie pans to keep the birds and other critters from eating the plants. So far they were working. She never understood why animals would snack on the good plants but leave the weeds alone. Weeding wasn't one of her favorite jobs, but it was necessary to keep the important plants—tomatoes, peas, beans, squash, cucumber, lettuce, and okra—healthy. They also had a few rows of corn planted near the field, but she didn't have to pay too much attention to those. The corn seemed to grow well despite the weeds.

As she tugged on a stubborn weed, she could hear Johnny and Sawyer out in the barnyard. She turned around to see a pitchfork full of dirty straw fly out of the chicken coop.

"Hey!" Johnny, who was standing by the door raking up the old straw into a pile, jumped back, the flying mass just missing him. "Watch where you're flinging that stuff."

Sawyer stepped inside the doorway of the coop. "Sorry. I'm not used to doing this, you know."

"I can tell." Johnny removed his straw hat and looked at the top and brim. He shook it out, then put it back on his head. "Aim your throws that way," he said, pointing to the growing pile a few feet away.

"Gotcha." Sawyer moved to go back inside, then poked his head out again. "It stinks in here."

Johnny grinned. "I know."

"Like, really bad."

"I *know*."

"You could have told me that before handing me the pitchfork."

"I could have. But I thought you'd want the true experience of cleaning out a chicken coop."

Sawyer made a face. "I think you didn't want to do it."

"That too."

Suddenly Sawyer smiled. It was the first time Mary Beth had seen him with anything but a scowl or uncertainty on his face. She couldn't help but smile herself. It was great to see him having fun, even if he was stuck working in the smelly coop.

Twenty minutes later the boys had the coop cleaned, and Mary Beth had finished weeding the garden. They both met her at the edge of the back deck. She wrinkled her nose as she looked at Sawyer. "You smell like the chickens."

"Hey, you know I've smelled worse." He smiled again.

Mary Beth laughed, glad to see he had a sense of humor. He seemed so different this afternoon, just like a normal kid, one she'd want to be friends with.

"Guess I need another pond bath." He looked at Johnny. "Are you up for a swim?"

"Sure."

Sawyer looked at Mary Beth. "You want to come?"

She hesitated. She had worked up a sweat in the garden, and the idea of plunging into the cool pond water really appealed to her. But she couldn't leave Micah alone. She had learned her lesson last time, when he had wandered off and scared them all to pieces. "I can't. But you two go."

"All right." Johnny tossed her his hat and started running. "Last one there is a rotten egg!"

"I already smell like a rotten egg," Sawyer hollered back, running after him.

Mary Beth walked inside, still grinning. She was glad to see Johnny and Sawyer getting along. She wasn't sure they would after their first couple of meetings. Now it seemed like they were becoming friends.

But what would happen when he left? They had to face that possibility, and soon. She couldn't keep sneaking things out to him. *Mami* was already suspicious, and Mary Beth didn't like doing things behind her back. It had been one thing to sneak off for a few hours every once in a while to her secret place, but now everything had changed. She needed some advice. But she couldn't go to her mother or father, not about this.

There was only one thing she could do in a situation like this. She had to pray.

She went upstairs, pausing by Micah's room. He stirred in his small bed, but didn't wake up completely. She went into her room and pulled out her journal, the one she had retrieved from the barn. She didn't have Sawyer's button anymore; she had sewed it back on his pants when she had washed them the other day. To keep *Mami* from finding out about the clothes, she had washed them in the bathroom sink, then took them back to the pond and laid them over a couple of tree branches to dry. Even though Sawyer had his own clothes back, he had chosen to wear Johnny's. That surprised her. The shirt she could understand; it was too hot to wear a sweatshirt. But he could have put on his jeans. They were stained but clean. Still, for some reason he chose to wear the Amish clothing.

Opening her journal, she picked up the pen by her bedside table and started to write. Sometimes she said her prayers silently, but occasionally she wrote them down. This prayer was important enough to record.

Dear God, please tell me what to do about Sawyer. I don't want him to run away again. He needs a family. Some people who care for him. But if I say anything, he'll take off. What should I do?

She closed the journal, then closed her eyes in silent prayer. A few moments later she heard Micah get up. While he had a plastic baby gate in the doorway of his room so he couldn't escape, she needed to go get him before he started crying. Saying a quick amen, she slid her journal under her bed and went to fetch her brother.

The rest of the afternoon went quickly. Johnny returned about an hour after he and Sawyer had gone swimming. His hair and pants were wet, but his shirt was partially dry. "Johnny, you're dripping on the floor."

"You know, you're sounding more and more like *Mami* every day."

She rolled her eyes and ignored his comment. "Where's Sawyer?"

"He left after we swam. Said he didn't want to take a chance on getting caught." Johnny shook his wet hair at her, splashing drops everywhere. Grinning, he dashed out of the room.

"Very funny, Johnny!" she hollered after him, then laughed.

A short while later Caleb showed up, his forearms red from being out in the sun all day. He'd worn his hat at least, sparing his cheeks from the sun. She had just started dinner when her mother came home, looking more relaxed than Mary Beth had seen her in a long time.

"How was your appointment?" Mary Beth asked as her mother walked into the room.

Mami took off her bonnet and laid it on the edge of the kitchen counter. She touched the sides of her *kapp*, then adjusted one of the bobby pins holding it in place. "*Gut*. The doctor says everything is fine. Thank goodness I'm starting to feel better. I'm not as sick as I first was." She walked over to Mary Beth and peered over her shoulder. "How's the tuna casserole working out?"

"*Gut*. I added a couple extra slices of cheese, just for *Daed*."

"Very nice. That will make you his favorite *dochder*."

She grinned. "That's because I'm his only *dochder*."

Her mother laughed. "That's true." She leaned over and looked inside the bowl holding the tuna fish and mushroom soup Mary Beth was mixing together. "Let's add some canned peas to that. Can you run downstairs and get them? I'll take over here." She took the wooden spoon from Mary Beth and began stirring the tuna and soup together.

Just as she made her way downstairs, she heard her mother call out her name. "Mary Beth?"

"*Ya?*"

"Bring up that leftover potato salad. We need to eat that up."

Mary Beth stilled. "Um, Johnny had it for lunch."

"Oh, that's fine. Just as long as it doesn't go to waste."

She let out a long breath and went downstairs. She definitely couldn't keep this up, and neither could Johnny.

Somehow they'd have to find another way to help Sawyer. She just had no idea how.

After supper, *Daed* took Micah and Caleb with him to visit a neighbor down the street. True to her word, *Mami* had shown Mary Beth how to pin the coat pattern onto the dark blue fabric, then cut it out. Mary Beth practiced for a while on scrap cloth while *Mami* went to lie down, tired from the long day.

With her parents and younger brothers occupied, Mary Beth thought it would be a good time to talk to Johnny about Sawyer. She carefully folded the thin tissue paper coat pattern and put it and her sewing materials away. She found her brother in the barn, standing on the edge of the pigpen, watching the animals eat their feed. She went and stood next to him.

"Thought I'd go see Sawyer in a few minutes," Johnny said. "You want to go?"

The pigs oinked and grunted as they shoved each other, trying to get the biggest share of food. "*Nee*. But you go on if you want."

"He's pretty cool." Johnny rose on his tiptoes on the edge of the pen. "Wasn't sure about him at first, though."

"Why not?"

"He wasn't real friendly, if you hadn't noticed."

"You wouldn't be all that friendly, either, if you had to live in a barn and didn't have enough to eat." She swatted at a fly buzzing between them.

"That's it, though. I didn't understand why he needed to live there. Why not just go home? Things can't be that bad."

"You remember what he said. About getting whipped on the hand. That sounds pretty bad to me."

"Yeah, but what if he made that up?" He turned to Mary Beth. "Do you think he's been lying to us all this time?"

She paused before answering. It hadn't dawned on her that Sawyer might lie to them. But now that Johnny had planted the seed in her in mind, doubts started to sprout. "What do you think?"

"I asked you first."

She reflected on everything that had happened during the past couple of weeks. Considering the way he was living, alone and with very little food, not to mention the awful state of his clothes and how skinny he was, he had to be telling the truth. No one would choose to live the way he was unless they had to. "*Nee*," she finally answered. "I don't think he's lying."

Johnny sighed. "Me either. Although part of me wishes he was lying. Doesn't seem right for him to lose his parents and not have anyone else care about him."

"I know. And I feel bad because I like him too. But we can't keep helping him like this."

He nodded. "*Mami* already told me to stop sneaking midnight snacks. I didn't know what she was talking about, but then I figured she saw the food missing. I had to pretend I was the one eating it so she wouldn't think something was up." He looked down at the pigs. "I don't like sneaking like this."

"But weren't you doing that before?"

His head popped up. "What?"

"You told me you'd been sneaking out of the house before we even met Sawyer. Remember?"

"*Ya*, but I didn't go anywhere. Sometimes I have trouble sleeping, so I go outside for a little while. Counting stars is a lot more interesting than counting sheep. Besides, if *Mami* or *Daed* had caught me, I would have told them what I was up to. So I say that's different."

"You still would have gotten in trouble."

"Not as much trouble as we're gonna get in if they find out about Sawyer." One of the pigs came up and sniffed the toe of Johnny's boot, then tried to bite it. He nudged it away and hopped down from the pen. He walked to the other side of the barn and sat down on a hay bale, blowing out a long breath. "So what are we gonna do?"

Mary Beth followed him. "I guess the only thing we can do is tell *Mami* and *Daed*."

He frowned. "You have another suggestion? Like one that won't get us grounded until next year?"

She sat down next to him. "Nope. That's all I could come up with."

"What if we took him to the Millers'? They have kids. Maybe they would know what to do."

"I don't know. They'd probably tell *Mami* and *Daed*, so we'd be back where we started."

"Maybe they wouldn't, if we asked them not to." Johnny rubbed his hands together. "They have that huge house— they might have room to keep him."

"It would be better than the barn," she agreed.

"Right."

She bit her bottom lip. "Do you think Sawyer would go? He might be afraid they'd call someone and send him back to his foster home."

"There's only one way to find out." Johnny stood up. "We'll ask him."

"Now?"

"*Ya.*"

She guessed now was as good a time as any. Like her brother said, her parents were busy and wouldn't notice if they were gone for a short while. "Okay, but we can't stay long."

"We won't."

They left the barn and walked through the backyard. They were on the edge of the property, heading toward the old barn, when their mother poked her head out of the window in their bedroom on the top floor. "Johnny? Mary Beth? Where are you two going?"

Mary Beth looked at Johnny, who had a panicked expression on his face. Their mother must have taken a very short nap. "Nowhere," he said, holding up his hands. "Me and Mary Beth were just walking around."

"Will you two go down by the pond and see if there are any ripe blueberries? I wanted to make a pie for your *daed* tomorrow."

She glanced at Johnny. "We can't go see Sawyer now," she whispered.

"I know. We'll have to talk to him tomorrow."

"Maybe we should talk to the Millers first? It wouldn't be fair to surprise them."

"Did you two hear me?" their mother repeated.

"*Ya*," Mary Beth said. "We'll go get some."

"*Danki*. Come inside and get a bowl out of the kitchen. That big yellow one in the top cupboard. When you fill it up, that will be enough." *Mami* ducked back inside the bedroom.

"I better go get the bowl," Mary Beth said.

But Johnny touched her arm, stopping her. "Are you sure we should talk to the Millers first?"

"I think so."

"But what would we say?" He appeared confused. "I don't think 'We've been helping out this Yankee boy hiding in that old abandoned barn no one's supposed to be in' is going to work."

Mary Beth frowned. Her brother was right. Maybe this was a bad idea. Never before had she felt so overwhelmed and confused. This problem was just getting bigger and bigger. She didn't know what to do.

"C'mon. We better get those blueberries before *Mami* thinks we're up to something." Johnny licked his lips. "Mmm, blueberry pie. We haven't had that in a long time."

Mary Beth liked blueberry pie too. And as they made their way to the blueberry patch near the pond, she was already trying to figure out a way to sneak a piece to Sawyer.

Nine

"My ride's here," *Daed* said as a car horn sounded outside. He wiped his mouth and beard with his napkin, then dropped it on the table and stood up.

Mary Beth poured a little more syrup over her blueberry pancakes. She and Johnny had picked extra yesterday. She looked at her *daed* with surprise. "Someone's taking you to work today?"

"*Ya*. Crackerjack needs new shoes. Cousin Aaron will be by this morning to put them on." He patted Micah on the head, then walked past *Mami* and touched her shoulder. "See you tonight."

"Bye, Daniel." *Mami* looked up at him and smiled; then he left for work.

Mary Beth quickly did her morning chores, then took Micah outside to play while *Mami* worked on her sewing. She pushed Micah in the tire swing for a little while, then gave him a small shovel and let him dig a hole in a small empty corner of the garden while she pulled a few more weeds. Tiny green tomatoes hung on the vines. She checked the sweet pea pods and saw that they would be ready to pick in a couple of weeks. The giant sunflowers she and her mother had planted along the edge of the garden were growing tall and sturdy.

"Da!" Micah said, flinging dirt behind him. Then he stuck both hands in the soil, lifted up his fists, and flung the dirt over his head.

"*Nee!*" Mary Beth ran over to him. Black dirt covered the shoulders of his short-sleeved blue shirt. She hadn't thought to put his small hat on, and now she wished she had, because he had dirt in his hair too. "Micah Mullet, why did you do that?"

"Da!" He looked up at her and smiled, then reached for more dirt. Before she could say anything, he threw it at her.

"Micah, *nee*—" Some of the dirt landed in her mouth. *Yuck!* "*Pfft!*" She blew it out. "Micah! That's naughty!"

Micah laughed, then stood up and started to run, his hands filled with dirt. Mary Beth dashed after him, ignoring the small clods of dirt hitting her ankles. "Ooh, get back here!"

"Da!" he said, laughing as he ran around the swing set. Mary Beth picked up speed, finally scooping him up in her arms.

"That's enough!" She took him in the house, even though he kept squirming in her arms. Then he started squalling as she headed for the bathroom. "You can cry all you want, but it's a bath for you," she said, taking him directly to the bathroom. She started the water in the tub.

Soon Micah was clean and ready for lunch. She fixed him his meal, then took him upstairs to take a nap. She stopped by the living room where her mother was sitting in a chair, threading a needle with black thread.

"Micah asleep?"

"*Ya*. I had to give him a bath before lunch because he dumped dirt on his head from the garden." She didn't mention that he'd also flung dirt in her mouth. *Ugh*. Just thinking about it made her want to spit.

Mami chuckled. "I heard the water running and figured he must have gotten into something. He's a pistol, that one. I think he'll be more lively than Caleb."

"Great," Mary Beth said flatly. "Just what we all need."

Mami looked up from her sewing, a disapproving look on her face. But a small smile played on her lips, and Mary Beth knew her *mami* understood. She pulled the thread through the needle's eye, then knotted the end with her index finger and thumb. "I thought I heard Aaron's buggy pull up while you were in the bathroom with Micah. Could you bring my purse? I'll give you the money to pay him for the shoes."

Mary Beth fetched her mother's purse and watched as *Mami* opened her wallet and pulled out a few bills. "This should cover it. If you need more, come back and let me know. Oh, and I have some oatmeal cookies for him to take over to his *mutter*. The plate belongs to Sarah."

Sarah Detweiler and her mother were first cousins,

which made Aaron Mary Beth's second cousin. She was also related to the Millers through marriage, as Aaron's sister was married to Moriah Miller's brother. Mary Beth thought the family relationships were confusing.

"I'll make sure he gets them." She took the money, then went to the kitchen and retrieved the cookies. As she walked outside, she saw their black buggy parked outside next to the barn, with Aaron's buggy standing beside it. As she passed her cousin's buggy, she peeked inside and saw a box of horse-shoes behind the bench seat. She set the plate of cookies on the seat. The foil covering would keep the bugs away.

She walked inside the barn, batting at two pesky horseflies buzzing around her head. Horseflies were a nuisance, and she could only imagine how annoyed the horses had to be with them. At the far end of the barn was Crackerjack's stall. The stall door was open, and she could hear the light plinking sound of the hammer against the small horseshoe nails.

She moved to stand by the stall door and watched quietly while Aaron worked. He wore a pair of brown leather pants split in the middle over his denim trousers. The horse stood behind him, and he had Crackerjack's foot bottom up between his knees. He bent over at the waist, holding a small nail in his mouth. Plucking it from between his lips, he put it in the hole of the shoe before pounding it in place.

Her cousin had been coming over for the past year or so, ever since he started working as a farrier for Gabe Miller. Mary Beth had seen Crackerjack shoed more than a few times, but each time she marveled that it didn't hurt the horse. Aaron had explained one time that the nail goes through the edge of the horse's hoof, which doesn't have any feeling. He said it was kind of like human toenails. And she knew Crackerjack would be worse off if he didn't wear shoes; with all the time he spent on the pavement and asphalt, his feet would be worn down to practically nothing.

She moved closer to Aaron and watched him work. He picked up the horse's left back foot and positioned it between his knees so he had access to the back of it. Then he took off the old shoe using a small metal bar that had a curve at the end. He yanked out the small nails, then took off the shoe and dropped it on the floor. Gunk coated the bottom of Crackerjack's hoof. Aaron took up another tool and started digging out the dirt from the horse's foot. Then he picked up a file and filed the back of the hoof smooth. "This is the last shoe. Can you hand it to me?"

She picked up the new shoe lying nearby and gave it to Aaron, who nailed it in place. Then he let the horse's foot down. Crackerjack whinnied and shook out his foot. "All done." Aaron looked up at her, sweat dripping down his face. He stood, slipped off his leather gloves, and wiped his forehead with the back of his hand. "How have you been, Mary Beth?"

"Okay."

"Just okay?" He peered down at her, as if he didn't believe her.

"*Ya.*" She fingered the ribbons on her *kapp* as she watched Aaron gather up his tools and the old horseshoes and nails.

As usual, Sawyer came to mind. The situation with him was all she could think about.

"Doesn't sound like things are okay." He looked down at her, his blue eyes searching her face. Damp locks of blond hair covered his forehead. When she didn't say anything, he motioned for her to follow him out of the stall, then shut the door behind her. He slung his tool bag over his shoulder and said, "Anything you want to talk about?"

"*Nee*. Not really."

"Okay. Then I'll be going." He started heading for the barn exit when she called out his name.

"Aaron?"

Turning around, he said, "*Ya?*"

"Can I ask you a question?" She didn't know what made her say that. She and Aaron had never been close. Too much of an age gap, for one thing. Also, he had left the community for a while when he was younger. Still, she couldn't stand not talking to someone else about Sawyer. Johnny didn't count, since he was as confused as she was. But could she trust Aaron? She wasn't completely sure, but now that she had his attention, she might as well find out.

He nodded. "Sure."

"Let's say you were keeping a secret about someone, and you really wanted to tell, but you thought you'd get into trouble if you did. What would you do?"

His blond brows furrowed together. "Hmm. I guess it depends on the secret. What kind of secret are you talking about?"

"Oh, just an old secret. Nothing special." She glanced down at the ground. "But if it was hard to keep that secret, even though someone asked you not to tell, would you say anything?"

Aaron leaned against the door frame of the barn. "Would someone be hurt or in trouble if you didn't say anything? Because if they would, then you should definitely say something." He looked at her for a moment as if he was waiting for her to comment. When she didn't, he continued. "Even if you might get in trouble over it."

Now she wished she hadn't brought it up with him. Even though he was telling her what she already knew, she really didn't want to hear it. "Okay," she said. "*Danki* for the advice."

"No problem."

"Oh, here," she said, handing him the bills. "Almost forgot. *Mami* said to give you this for payment for the shoes. There are also some cookies for your *mutter* in your buggy."

"*Danki.*" Aaron took the bills from her, looked at them for a moment, then gave one back. "Give this back to your *mutter*. Tell her she overpaid me."

"Are you sure?" Mary Beth looked at the bill in his hand. It wasn't like *Mami* to make a mistake like this. She and her father always knew where every penny went.

"I'm sure." He pressed the bill in her hand. "Tell her I said hello and that I'll try to stop inside another time. I need to get over to Christian Weaver's before noon."

With a nod, Mary Beth took the other bill back. She

walked out with Aaron and watched him climb into the buggy. Once he left, she thought about what he'd said and sighed. She was tired of worrying about all this. Aaron was right. She couldn't go on keeping this secret much longer. Mary Beth went inside and handed her mother the twenty-dollar bill.

"What's this?" *Mami* said, looking up at her.

"Aaron said you overpaid him."

Mami put down her sewing and looked at the bill in Mary Beth's outstretched hand. "*Nee*. I paid him exactly the amount he and your father agreed on." She kept staring at the bill, then took it from Mary Beth. "*Danki*," she said quietly, looking away.

Mary Beth noticed a quiver in her mother's voice. "Are you all right?"

She looked at Mary Beth, her eyes shining. "*Ya*. I'm fine. Just thankful to be blessed with such a generous family. God is so very *gut* to us." She wiped underneath her eyes and put the bill in her purse. "Speaking of our brethren, we're going to be busy the rest of the week. We're hosting church a week from this Sunday. So I'll need you and your brothers to help me get ready. The house needs to be clean—"

"It already is," Mary Beth interjected, knowing what her mother was about to say. She didn't see how they could possibly get the house any cleaner.

But *Mami* sure could. "I mean really clean, not just tidy. Spotless. Especially the basement—that's where we'll have the service. We'll also have to do some baking. And some . . ."

Mary Beth tuned out her mother's voice as she continued to make a list of the things they had to do to get ready for church in ten days. The days leading up to hosting church were always busy, as everything had to be perfect and pass her mother's inspection, since they only hosted church once a year. Next week she wouldn't have much time, if any, to sneak over to the barn and talk to Sawyer. They would be lucky if they could drop off food in the box by the pond. Maybe she or Johnny could sneak over in the middle of the night, but she really didn't want to do that anymore. She chewed on her bottom lip. This was all getting too complicated.

"Mary Beth, are you listening to me?"

Mary Beth turned her focus back on her mother. *"Ya, Mami.* I heard what you said. Don't worry, we'll get everything ready in time for church."

"I know you will." She smiled. "I promise you won't be stuck doing all the work. Johnny and Caleb are going to have to do their fair share."

Mary Beth was definitely glad to hear that. She smiled too.

"Thought that might make you happy." She gestured for Mary Beth to sit down on the couch by her chair. Once Mary Beth was seated, she said, "You and I really haven't had a chance to talk about the *boppli.* I hope you're excited about the baby coming, but I would understand if you weren't."

"I am excited, *Mami.*"

Her mother tilted her head to the side. "You don't have to pretend, Mary Beth. Are you worried about having another brother?"

She started to deny it, but her mother already knew the truth. *"Ya.* A little."

"I know it's hard having such lively brothers. They're a lot different than you are. Even though you and Johnny are twins, you're still opposites in a lot of things." She reached out and touched Mary Beth's hand. "You're a lot like me when I was a girl."

"I am?"

Mami nodded. "Your *onkel* Wally used to drive me crazy. He's just like Johnny, only he liked to play practical jokes. Like the time he put a frog in my bed."

Mary Beth made a face. *"Eww.* Was it slimy?"

"I don't know, because as soon as my toe touched it, I jumped out of bed!" She laughed. "He got in a lot of trouble for that, but it didn't stop him from playing more tricks on me."

It was hard to believe that her responsible, serious uncle had been such a prankster. Maybe there was hope for Johnny after all.

The rest of the week and the next went by quickly, as Mary Beth and her mother were busy baking and getting the house ready for church that Sunday, while her brothers were cleaning up the yard. She and Johnny took turns dropping off food in the crate by the pond, but Sawyer was never there when it was her turn. Johnny said he hadn't seen him either, but whenever they checked the crate, the food was gone.

She wondered what he did all day. Surely he didn't stay in the barn. Maybe he explored the woods nearby. She couldn't imagine what else he might be doing, other than sneaking into other people's yards. She didn't like that idea at all. If he got caught, it would be worse for him than if she and Johnny had told their parents.

Sunday morning arrived, and with it hot, muggy weather. It didn't take long for their driveway and yard to fill up with black buggies. After the three-hour church service was over, everyone came up from the basement and prepared to eat, with most of the kids going outside to play in the yard or in the Millers' adjacent field.

Mary Beth couldn't join them because she had to help her mother in the kitchen. They weren't the only two getting the meal ready for everyone. There were several other women, too, including *Mami*'s cousin Sarah, Aaron's mother. She had caught a glimpse of Aaron earlier, talking with Elisabeth Byler after church in the living room. The way they stood close as they talked made her think they were sweet on each other.

Everyone had brought something to share, so Mary Beth was mostly stuck doing dishes at the sink. And boy, were there a lot of them. She didn't think she would ever get out of the kitchen.

A couple of hours later, most everyone had left to go home, and Mary Beth was finally able to fill her plate with food and go outside. Katherine hadn't stayed for the fellowship because her mother was home sick and her father wanted the family to get back home, so Mary Beth found herself alone. She decided to go sit by the pond and enjoy her late lunch in peace.

She sat down on a flat rock near the edge of the pond. Even though the air was sticky and hot, being in the fresh air was a welcome relief from being cooped up in the kitchen. She had left her shoes in the house and now dug her toes into the cool earthen bank of the pond. In the fall her father let the grass grow tall around it, but they kept it short in the summer. Out of habit she checked on the crate behind another large rock on the opposite side of the pond. There was nothing in it. She hoped Johnny had brought Sawyer something from all the food today. Sawyer would have a good meal if he had.

She sat back down on the rock and bowed her head, saying a silent prayer. The sun warmed her and cast a reflection on the pond's smooth surface. A trickle of sweat slid down her back, but she ignored it. She spied a small frog jumping into the water, causing a few waves to ripple from the shore toward the center of the pond. As she bit into her sandwich, she listened to a cow lowing in the distance. *Ah. Peace and quiet. Finally.*

"Hey."

Her head shot up. Sawyer stood next to the pond, his hands in the pockets of Johnny's old pants. He shook his head to the side to get his sweaty bangs out of his eyes. His cheeks looked red, as if they were sunburned.

"Hi." Her brows lifted. "I'm surprised to see you." Although her parents were back at the house relaxing after a busy day, there was still the risk her father or Caleb might come back here. She hadn't expected Sawyer to risk getting caught, but here he was.

"Haven't seen you around much," he said.

"We had church this week, so I've been busy."

"Had church?"

She nodded. "All the families in the district alternate between having church in their homes every other Sunday. It was our turn this week."

"So you don't have a special building you go to?"

She shook her head. "Nope. And we had a lot of work to do. But Johnny and I have been taking turns leaving stuff for you."

"I know." He moved and sat down beside her on the rock, wiping his forehead with the back of his hand. "Thanks." He picked up a twig, then twirled it between his fingers as he stared at the pond. "Really hot out here. It would be a good day for a swim."

"Is that why you're here? If so, I'd wait until later. *Daed* and Caleb have been known to swim out here a time or two during the day when it's really hot."

"I didn't come out here to swim, but thanks for the warning." He snapped the twig in half. "I've been watching you guys the past couple days."

"You have?"

"From a distance. When I get bored I come over here and see what you all are up to. You really have a lot of chores, you know?"

"Not any more than most kids."

"Most Amish kids." He tossed the two stick pieces into the murky pond water. "I don't know any American kids who work that hard."

"American?"

"Yeah. Isn't that right? You're Amish, we're American."

"We're American too," Mary Beth said, almost laughing. "You're a Yankee. That's what we call people who aren't Amish."

He shrugged. "Same difference."

They didn't say anything for a long moment. Then Mary Beth turned to him. "You know, you never told me about how you got here to Middlefield. Or where you're from."

He dug his big toe into the ground. "I know."

"How come?"

Sawyer let out a long breath. "I didn't know if I could trust you or not."

"And now?"

Pausing for a moment, he said, "I trust you."

"Enough to tell me?"

After another long pause he nodded. "Yeah."

Mary Beth was glad he felt confident enough to tell her his story. Still, he didn't start talking right away. So she asked him a question to get him started. "What happened to your parents?"

"They were killed in a car wreck. My mom's car broke down on the way home from work over a year ago. She called my dad to come pick her up. As they were driving home, they were struck by a drunk semitruck driver." He stared down at the ground. "They were dead at the scene."

Hearing the sadness in his voice made her regret bringing it up. She thought he might not say anything else, but then he opened his mouth and spoke.

"After they died I went to a group home for boys. They assigned me a social worker, and then they searched for my relatives. They found an uncle, but he was in prison. There were a couple of older cousins, but they all live in Wisconsin. None of them were willing to take me anyway, so I had to stay in the group home until they found a foster family who would take me in."

"Did it take long to find one?"

"A few weeks. I actually went to a couple of them. The first one was okay, but out of the blue they decided they didn't want to foster kids anymore. So they sent me back. I was at the group home for another month before they found another family." He stood up and walked to the edge of the pond. His back to her, he said, "I stayed there nine months; then I couldn't take it anymore. That's when I ran away."

"What happened?" She bit her bottom lip as soon as the question left her mouth. "Never mind. I shouldn't have asked."

He turned around, his expression dead serious. "Let's just say they weren't the nicest people on the planet. My foster dad really liked using his belt, and not just to hold up his pants."

"Wow."

"Yeah. Wow." He looked off into the distance, emotion-less. Then she saw him swallow, and she knew he had to be hurting inside.

"How did you get here, then?"

"I was living in Painesville." He looked at her again. "Do you know where that is?"

She shook her head.

"I think it's about an hour or so from here, but I'm not really sure. When I left the foster home, I hopped in the back of this guy's pickup truck. I didn't care where he took me. I just wanted to get out of there. I remember going on a freeway, and after that I fell asleep. When he pulled into a gas station, I jumped out and ran away into some woods. I kept walking until I got here." He stuffed his hands in his pockets and looked at her. "It was almost night when I found the barn, and I was exhausted. I went inside and slept. When I woke up the next morning, I saw all your stuff—the food, juice, and blanket. It was more than I'd had in a few days, so I decided to stay. And now here I am. End of story."

He moved closer to her, his gaze darting to her plate. She noticed and held it out to him. It was loaded with a roast beef sandwich, cheesy potato casserole, a corn muffin, and three cookies. "Want some? I took way too much. I can't eat it all."

He shook his head but still looked at her plate.

"Go on."

"I've taken enough from you."

Picking up the corn muffin, she handed it to him. "I

don't mind. Thanks for telling me your story. I'm sorry you had to go through such a hard time."

He shrugged, then took the muffin from her. "It's life. Mmm. Who made this?"

"Mrs. Miller. She and her family live over there." She pointed across the field in the direction of the Millers' house.

"Oh. I thought maybe you made it."

"*Nee*. Just the cookies."

"You like to cook?"

"It's better than babysitting my brothers."

"Yeah, you don't like your brothers too much, do you?"

Mary Beth looked at him, frowning. "What makes you say that?"

His face turned red and he looked away. "I think you've mentioned it before."

"I don't think I've said anything about my brothers, except for Johnny." She turned and stared at him. "Tell me the truth. How do you know?"

He cast her a quick look. "I, um . . ."

"You what?"

"I . . ." He looked away.

"Just tell me!" Mary Beth glared at him.

"Fine." Sawyer glared back. "I read your journal, okay?"

She clenched the paper plate. Any pity she'd had suddenly evaporated. "What?"

"Look, I was bored, and there was nothing else to do. If you didn't want anyone reading it, you shouldn't have left it there."

She dropped the plate and stood up, putting her hands on her hips. "I left it there because I didn't think anyone would find it and read it." Her cheeks flamed as she thought about the private thoughts she'd written. How annoying Caleb was, what a jerk Johnny could be, and how Micah always wanted her attention. But worse, she had written about Christopher. Pages and pages about how cute he was, how much she liked him. How she wished one day they would get married. She'd even decorated a page with hearts and wrote her and Christopher's names in the center. Sawyer had read all that.

He had also seen her drawings. She had never shown anyone her artwork. Like her writings, her art was private and personal. Not intended for anyone else's eyes. Definitely not for Sawyer's.

Humiliation washed over her. She'd never been so embarrassed. Or so angry. "I can't believe you did this to me. After everything we've done for you—"

"Wait a minute! I never asked you to do anything for me." Sawyer jumped up from the rock. "You're the one who keeps saying that God would want you to help me out. But the minute you get mad, you're throwing it back in my face."

"That's not what I'm doing."

"Yeah, it is. If that's the way it's gonna be, then I don't need you or your brother anymore." He glowered at her. "I never should have stayed here in the first place. That was my biggest mistake."

"*Nee*. Your biggest mistake was running away."

"That was the one thing I did right! Then I had to screw it all up by coming here." He turned around and walked away.

"Well, fine!" Not only was her pride picked, but her feelings were hurt too. He'd read her private thoughts, and now he was mad because she was upset. If anyone had a right to be angry, it was her, not Sawyer! "You can forget about us helping you anymore."

"I don't need your help!" He ran off, disappearing into the woods near the pond.

She plopped back down on the rock and looked at her nearly full plate of food, still angry and fighting for calm. She'd lost her appetite and her friendship with Sawyer in less than ten minutes. That had to be some kind of record.

Sawyer ran back to the barn and flung off the Amish clothes he'd been wearing for the past few days. They had actually been more comfortable than his own clothes, which surprised him. But he wouldn't be obligated to Mary Beth one second longer. Not if she was going to act like an idiot over her stupid journal. Especially after everything he'd told her. He'd thought she understood. And for a moment, he had seen compassion on her face. He didn't want anyone to feel sorry for him, yet it was nice to know that at least someone cared. But like everything else in his life, that didn't last long.

It was already steaming hot in the barn, and he started to sweat as soon as he slipped on his hot clothes. He didn't care. He needed to leave Middlefield as soon as possible, and he couldn't do that wearing Amish clothes. He might blend in with all the Amish people here, but once he got beyond the town limits, he would be noticed right away. Although, now that he thought about it, someone might think it was strange he was wearing a sweatshirt in the middle of July. But there was nothing he could do about that.

He dropped to the ground, raising his knees up and putting his forearms over them. He dangled his head between his legs and let out a heavy breath. Sweat rolled down the top of his nose. No matter what he did, he couldn't win. The time he'd spent here had made him feel better than he had since his parents died. Being around Mary Beth and Johnny had chased away the loneliness.

Well, he'd been foolish to think it would last forever. And the way Mary Beth looked when he left, he didn't doubt she probably ran right back inside to tell her parents about him.

The thought terrified him. He couldn't go back to that foster family. He pulled up the sleeve of his sweatshirt and looked at the souvenir of his time there, something he had managed to hide from both Johnny and Mary Beth—a round burn made by a cigarette. Neither his foster mother nor father had done that, but one of their son's friends had. "Don't you ever let anyone see that," his foster mother had spit when she saw it, blowing her sour breath in his face. "We got a good deal going here, and I don't want you to blow it."

He shut his eyes against the memory, shoving it away.

He rose to his feet and glanced around the barn, his home for the past five weeks. He needed to leave now, but his feet wouldn't move. For the first time since he'd left the foster home, he was scared. Before, he had just run away, knowing he had to get out of his situation. But now things were different. He knew he had to go.

Problem was, he didn't want to.

He thought about his conversations with Mary Beth. She really believed there was a God who cared about her, and about him. About everyone, it seemed. Yet after what he'd been through, how could he understand that? Or even accept it? Where had God been when his parents died? When he'd been in the group home? When that punk teenager had put out a cigarette on his arm?

Shaking his head, he walked out the door, leaving the barn behind. He couldn't depend on anyone but himself. Especially not a God who let terrible things happen. That was a fact he could accept. As he headed into the woods near the barn, he glanced up at the sky. Dark, angry-looking clouds had started to form, and the heat was more oppressive than ever. It looked as if it might storm. Great. A rainy night in the woods with only trees as shelter. The bad luck just kept on coming.

He turned around and looked back at the barn. It would be so easy to walk back inside, to ride out the rain in a place where he felt safe. Water would fall through the holes in the roof, but he would stay warm enough. Over the past month, the barn had become his sanctuary.

But he couldn't go back. If he didn't leave now, he would

never leave, until he was discovered and taken by force. And if he stayed, that was exactly what would happen.

Turning around, he ran toward the woods as the first sound of thunder boomed in the distance.

Ten

MARY BETH lay in her bed. She couldn't sleep. Her argument with Sawyer kept replaying in her mind. She wasn't nearly as upset now as she had been when she first found out he'd read her journal. But she couldn't forget the angry look on Sawyer's face when he stalked off, telling her he didn't need them anymore. Did that mean he was leaving Middlefield? Where would he go? He had no money, only the clothes on his back. What would he eat? Where would he sleep?

Her mind whirred with worry, and she couldn't take it anymore. Swinging her legs over the side of her bed, she stood up and snuck into Johnny's room. Careful not to wake up Caleb, who was snoring loudly in his bed, she nudged her twin on the shoulder. Once. Twice. "Johnny," she whispered, shoving his shoulder a little harder. "Johnny, wake up!"

He rolled over. She couldn't see his face in the darkness, but she hoped he was awake. When he sat up on his elbows, she knew he was. "I'm up, Mary Beth. Good grief. I've been up. Who can sleep in this heat?"

"Then why were you ignoring me?"

"Because I can?" He paused. "Sorry. Heat's making me grouchy."

"Look, Johnny, we have to tell *Mami* and *Daed* about Sawyer. Now."

"Tell them in the middle of the night? Are you *ab im kopp*? You're just mad because he read your journal."

Mary Beth's mouth dropped open. "How do you know that?"

"I overheard you guys talking by the pond today. I was going to join you, but then you had to go and get mad at him. It's just a stupid journal. I would have done the same thing eventually and you know it."

"That doesn't make it right!" What was wrong with these boys that they thought it was okay to invade her privacy? She would never do that to them.

"That doesn't matter right now. I still think we should wait to tell them. I've been thinking about the Millers again—"

"We've already talked about this."

"Just hear me out." She heard him move, and from what she could tell he was now sitting up. "Sawyer's been telling me a few things about what happened to him in the foster home."

"I know. He told me some of it today. Before I got mad at him."

"Then you know he can't go back there. We have to help him find a way to stay here. In Middlefield."

"And how's that going to happen?"

"We have to find someone to help us, but not *Mami* and *Daed*."

"Why not? Johnny, I'm tired of keeping this secret. Maybe they would understand."

"I don't think so. What do you think they're gonna do if we tell them about him? Let him live with us?"

Mary Beth hadn't thought of that possibility. But why not? She knew money would be an issue. But time and time again she'd heard her parents say, "God provides." And he always did. If God wanted Sawyer to live with them, he would make it happen.

Caleb suddenly snorted. Mary Beth and Johnny stilled. She hoped her brother hadn't been awake the whole time they'd been talking. Then she heard the rustle of sheets, and Caleb started snoring again.

"I think we should ask them," she said, lowering her voice.

"Ask who what?"

"Ask *Mami* and *Daed* about Sawyer living with us."

Before he could answer, a crack of thunder sounded outside. It had been threatening for the past few hours. She had even heard a few rumbles earlier in the evening, but the sky remained dry. "We'll never know unless we try."

"*Nee*. I don't want to take the risk."

"Talking to the Millers is risky too."

He didn't say anything for a long moment. Then he sighed. "I know."

A flash of lightning illuminated the bedroom, followed by another loud thunder boom. "Johnny, if we explain to *Mami* and *Daed* about Sawyer, they'll understand. They'll know why we had to sneak out and help him. And when they find out how terrible his life was with his foster parents, they'll want to help him too. Even if they say he can't live here, they might figure out a way to keep him from going back to foster care." She stood up from the side of his bed. "You know we have to do this. We don't have any other choice."

He didn't say anything for a long while. "Fine," he said, sounding more than a little reluctant. "But not tonight. I don't want to wake them up. You know how crabby *Daed* gets when that happens. Let's wait until tomorrow, when he gets home from work. After supper, he's usually in a *gut* mood."

She didn't really want to wait, but she knew that was the smart thing to do. "All right." Turning to leave, another round of lightning flashed in the sky. She jumped at the echoing thunder that immediately followed it.

Johnny clambered out of bed and went to the window. His profile was lit up by another strike of lightning. "Whoa," he said in a loud whisper.

Mary Beth joined him. Lightning bolts streaked the sky, some of them shooting down to the ground in the distance. Still, there was no rain, but it had to be coming soon, especially with a storm like this. The window was open, and the air outside was thick and heavy with moisture.

"That's some electrical storm," Johnny said. "It's pretty, in a creepy sort of way." Thunder sounded again and he flinched.

"You don't think it's gonna hit the house, do you?"

"Nah. Lightning doesn't strike houses. Just trees. And people, if you're in the middle of a field."

"Who told you that?"

"Dan. Said his cousin got hit by lightning last year. His hair caught on fire and everything." Johnny leaned against the window, folding his arms and putting them on the ledge.

"And you believe him?"

"Why not? It's a neat story."

Mary Beth shook her head. Dan had been known to stretch the truth more than a time or two. "That doesn't make much sense. Why would lightning not strike a house but hit trees and people?"

"I don't know. Ask Dan."

"Forget it. I'm going to bed."

"Hang on a minute. Don't get any bright ideas of talking to *Mami* and *Daed* without me," he said, turning to look at her. "I mean it. We need to do this together. They won't be nearly as mad if we both tell at the same time."

"I'm not going to, don't worry. I don't want to get in trouble any more than you do." Spinning on her heel, she walked out of the room and padded down the hall.

A few moments later she climbed into bed. It was too hot for covers. It was even too hot for sleep.

As another roll of thunder ricocheted through her ears, she thought about Sawyer. If it was this loud in the house, it had to be ten times louder outside. The old barn had too many gaps and holes in the walls to muffle the noise. And if he wasn't in the barn . . .

Johnny's story entered her mind. Sawyer couldn't get struck by lightning, could he? She'd never known that to happen to anyone, despite what Daniel said. But still, was it possible?

She blinked as a flash of lightning lit up the room. Closing her eyes, she started to pray.

Just as she started to drift off, she heard the sound of a dog barking. At first it sounded faint, but then it became louder. Opening her eyes, she realized the barking was coming from under her window. She jumped out of bed, looked outside, and saw a black-and-white shaggy dog. *Roscoe.*

"*Shh,*" she yelled in a loud whisper. "Roscoe, stop! You'll wake *Mami* and *Daed.*" But the dog kept barking, then twirled around in a circle and barked again. Mary Beth put her hands on top of her head. "Roscoe, hush!"

"What's he doing?" Johnny asked, coming up behind her. He looked down at Roscoe. "Why is he barking like that?"

"I don't know. I've never heard him bark before."

"He's got to shut up before he wakes everyone up."

"I know. I yelled at him, but he won't listen."

Johnny dashed out of her room and she followed, trying to move as fast as she could without making noise. The lightning flashes continued, followed by angry-sounding thunder. Roscoe's barks became louder. What in the world was wrong with that dog?

She followed Johnny into the kitchen and to the back

door. He opened it up, ignoring the creak, and they both walked outside. "Shut up, you *dumm* dog!"

"Johnny! Don't call him that."

"You got a better way to quiet him down?"

"Being mean to him won't work!"

"I'm not being mean . . . Hold on." He lifted his head and sniffed. "You smell that?"

"Smell what?"

"Smoke." He sniffed a few more times, then sped down the steps. Roscoe stood beside him, still barking, now in the direction of the field. "I smell smoke."

Mary Beth breathed in. For a moment all she could smell was the impending rain, but then she caught a whiff of something else. Johnny was right, something was burning. She whirled around and looked at the barn several yards away. Now that she had detected the smell, it seemed to grow stronger. "Johnny, what if it's the barn?"

"It's not the barn. The smell would be stronger."

"Not if the fire just started." Her heart skipped at the thought of Crackerjack and the pigs being caught in a blaze. Roscoe came up to her and continued to bark.

"Calm down," Johnny said. "I'll check it out, but I'm sure it's nothing."

"I'm coming with you."

"It'll only take a minute. Stay here." Another bolt of lightning flashed across the sky.

"But what if there's a fire? You can't handle that all by yourself. You'll need my help."

"If there's a fire, I'll holler and let you know. Then you go get *Daed*." He started off toward the barn.

He had no right to boss her around. She ran after him, jumping at the thunder that seemed to rumble all around her. Being out in the open while the lightning flashed and the thunder boomed scared her. When she got to the barn, she ran inside, grateful for the shelter. She let Roscoe in and slammed the door. At least he had stopped barking.

Johnny had lit the lantern hanging on the hook near the door. Now he turned and faced her. "I thought I told you to stay at the house!"

"And I told you I wasn't letting you come out here alone." She looked around the barn, checking everything out. The pigs were grunting, gathering at the edge of the gate, expecting to be fed even though it was the middle of the night. Crackerjack let out a whinny and stomped his feet as he stood in his stall. She couldn't smell any smoke and didn't see any flames. Her shoulders relaxed a little. "No fire here, thank goodness."

"None in the chicken coop either. But the animals aren't too happy."

"We disturbed their sleep."

"I don't think that's the reason." Johnny cowered at another boom of thunder. "They don't like the weather any more than we do."

"You're probably right." The pigs continued to huddle by the gate, and she wasn't sure it was only because they wanted to be fed.

The heat had made the pigpen even smellier than usual, the stink of their muck turning Mary Beth's stomach. She opened up the barn door and breathed in a lungful of fresh air. Just as she did, Roscoe started barking. She also noticed the smoke smell again, this time even stronger.

"Johnny!" She gestured for him to come over.

A worried look appeared on his face. "But where's the fire? It's not the house, barn, or coop."

Forgetting her fear, she took a few steps outside and looked around. Then she glanced at the field next to their house, the one she crossed to get to the old barn. Another bolt of lightning flashed, lighting up the sky. Her stomach dropped to her knees at what she saw. She pointed at the old barn. "Look!"

Johnny rushed out to join her. "What? I don't see anything."

"The old barn's on fire! I just saw smoke coming out of it."

"Are you sure? I can't see anything in the dark."

"*Ya*! When the lightning flashed I saw it." She looked at him, frightened. "What if Sawyer is in there?"

"If he was, I'm sure he got out before the fire got too bad."

"But what if he didn't? What if he's trapped in there?"

Roscoe barked one more time, then ran off toward the field.

"C'mon!" She grabbed Johnny's wrist and yanked on it. "We have to find out!"

Johnny pulled his wrist free, but he followed Mary Beth as she ran across the field. As they approached the barn, Mary Beth's heart pounded. The barn was engulfed in flames. The field surrounding it had been spared, but who knew how long it would be before the fire spread? "Sawyer!" Mary Beth called out his name while she closed the distance as fast as she could.

They both stopped short a few feet from the barn. Flames licked up the warped sides and threw off waves of heat. Could anyone survive in there? Roscoe barked non-stop. "Sawyer!" she yelled again, running to the other side of the barn. Each time she got too close, the heat forced her to back away.

"Johnny! Mary Beth!" They heard their *daed* yelling behind them.

Shocked to hear his voice, Mary Beth turned around to see her father rushing toward them, holding a flashlight in his good hand. A few heavy raindrops started to fall, pelting her nightgown as she ran toward him. "The barn—it's on fire!" The words were almost stuck in her throat, and she started coughing from the smoke.

The flames illuminated *Daed*'s face. He looked at Johnny. "Run to the neighbors and call the fire department."

Mary Beth screamed, "We have to save him!"

"Save who?" He looked at Johnny, who hadn't left yet. Her brother seemed frozen in place. "Johnny, *geh!*" *Daed* shouted. "Now, before the fire gets out of control."

Johnny darted away. Mary Beth had never seen him run

so fast. She turned around and headed for the barn, intent on seeing if Sawyer was there.

"Stop!" *Daed* reached out and grabbed her arm. "Where do you think you're going?"

"I have to see if he's in there."

Her father grimaced. "Mary Beth, what are you talking about? Who's in the barn?"

Suddenly the sky opened up and torrents of rain fell down. Her *daed*'s shoulders slumped a bit. "Thank the Lord," he said, letting go of her arm. "The rain will help put out the fire." His hair started to plaster against his head.

Mary Beth ignored the downpour, despite the driving rain roaring in her ears. She looked at the barn, still engulfed in flames. Smoke plumed in the air, and she started to cough again.

Suddenly she saw Roscoe dash into the burning barn. "Roscoe!" she screamed. She started after him, but her father grabbed her again. He turned and gripped her shoulders.

"Mary Beth! You can't go after him!"

Tears ran down her face. "Why did he run in there? Why?"

Her father pulled her into his embrace. "I don't know."

She cried against her father's chest. The barn was almost completely consumed by fire. Nothing could survive in there. She knew it. Unable to stop herself, she turned to look.

Just then Roscoe came running out, a piece of cloth dangling from his mouth.

Flying out of her father's arms, she ran to the dog and

hugged him. "Thank God you're safe!" She put her face in his neck and breathed in the smoke, not caring that it made her throat burn. Then she pulled back and looked at what he was holding in his mouth.

"What is this?" *Daed* knelt down beside them.

When Mary Beth grasped the cloth, Roscoe let go. She looked at it, recognizing the dark blue denim. "Johnny's old pants." She felt like she'd been punched in the chest.

"What?" *Daed* took the cloth from her. "What were Johnny's pants doing in the barn?"

But she couldn't answer him. All she could do was cry. Sawyer had been in there. He hadn't taken off Johnny's clothes since she had given them to him. The cloth was singed at the edges. She closed her eyes against the horror of what had happened as the rain drenched her body.

Johnny appeared, out of breath. He was soaked, his clothes molded to his body as if they were glued on. "They're on their way," he said in between gasps of air. Then he started to cough.

"We have to get you two away from here." *Daed* put one arm around Mary Beth and one around Johnny and led them away from the barn, Roscoe dogging their heels. When Mary Beth started to protest, he gripped her shoulder tighter.

"Don't argue with me, Mary Beth. You will do as I say." Mary Beth had to comply. They moved away from the smoke but stayed close enough to watch the burning barn. A hissing sound filled the air as some of the fire was extinguished by the rain. In the distance she heard the loud wail of fire sirens, and within moments the firefighters had pulled up, bringing their long red fire truck and a smaller red truck close behind them. They jumped out of the fire truck and immediately went to get their hoses.

A man in a yellow firefighter's suit came up to them. "Is this your barn?"

"*Nee*," *Daed* replied. "It's been abandoned for years. I'm surprised it hasn't burned down before now."

"So there was nothing inside? No animals we need to get out?"

He shook his head. "*Nee*, there's nothing in there. Not anymore."

Mary Beth started to sob. She looked at Johnny, who also had tears in his eyes.

"Mary Beth," her father said, putting his arm around her again. "Don't cry. The dog's okay. Everything is all right. It's just an old barn."

"It's not just an old barn!" she cried. "Sawyer was in there, and now he's—he's—" She fought to speak but couldn't.

"Sawyer? Who's Sawyer?" Her father looked at Johnny. "What's she talking about?"

Johnny wiped his nose. "A boy we know." His voice sounded thick. "He was living in the barn."

The firefighter sprang into action. "Why didn't you say something before?" He took off toward the barn, yelling instructions to the other men. He pulled on a bulky mask with a clear shield and ran inside. Mary Beth hiccupped as she watched them.

Her father bent down in front of Mary Beth and looked her in the eye. "No one's supposed to be in the barn. It's condemned."

She didn't answer her father. Instead she stared at the fire, which was slowly going out now, with the help of the rain and the firefighters. She tried to pray that the firefighters would miraculously bring Sawyer out alive, but she held out little hope. Maybe he'd really left Middlefield this time. But he had threatened to go several times before. She had a hard time believing he had now.

After several long, agonizing moments, the firefighters emerged from the building. One of them approached, and she could see it was the same firefighter they had spoken to before. He pulled up his mask. "There's no one in there," he said, looking at Mary Beth directly. "Are you sure there was someone there when the fire started?"

"I—I don't know." She looked down at the ground, then back at the firefighter. She sniffed. "I wasn't sure if he was there or not."

"Well, if he was there before, he's not now," the firefighter said. "At least as far as we can tell."

Mary Beth leaned against her father.

"I have to get back," the fireman said. "But don't go anywhere; I'll have some questions for you."

Johnny moved to stand beside her and their father, and

they both glanced up at him, expecting him to be angry. Instead he remained quiet. All three of them continued watching in silence as the firefighters finished their job. The rain had let up but was still coming down in steady, light drops. Mary Beth folded her arms across her chest as water dripped down her nose. Her long hair, unbound, hung down her back in heavy, soggy waves.

When the fire was completely out, the firemen wrapped up their hoses. Their firefighter approached them one last time. "Do you have any idea who owns the barn?"

"A Yankee family, but I never met them," their *daed* said. "It's been deserted for a long time, before my family and I moved here."

"All right. I'll check with city hall, then. I'm sure they have a record of ownership." He looked at Mary Beth. "Once we got the fire out, we went back inside. You're right, someone was there at one time. We saw a couple of pop cans, along with a thermos and a half-burned blanket." He took in a deep breath. "We still can't say for sure if anyone was caught in the fire or not."

Mary Beth nodded, wiping away the rain pelting her face.

"Did you know the person who could have been in there?" the fireman asked.

Mary Beth hesitated, looking at Johnny. He nodded slowly. "*Ya.*" She didn't dare look at her father. "I did."

"We both did," Johnny chimed in.

"Who was it?"

"His name is Sawyer. He's a Yankee, but not from here."

"He ran away," Johnny added. "He was hiding out in the barn for a few weeks."

The firefighter nodded, but he looked concerned. "Why didn't you tell anyone about this?"

Mary Beth didn't reply, only shrugged. She didn't have a good excuse—and now, looking back, not even a good reason. They should have said something long ago. If they had, this wouldn't have happened.

The firefighter frowned, his thick black eyebrows forming a V above his eyes. "Next time don't keep that information to yourself. What's his last name?"

Johnny sniffed, then wiped off the water dripping from his nose. "We don't know."

The fireman looked at their father. "Sir, I'm going to have to tell the police about this. We'll operate on the assumption he's alive and hiding out somewhere else. They'll put out a search for him. Hopefully they'll find him soon and take him back where he belongs."

Mary Beth sucked in a breath. "Are we going to jail?" A quick glance at Johnny told her he was thinking the same thing.

For the first time since he arrived, the firefighter's expression softened. "No. You won't go to jail. But the police will have questions for both of you. This boy needs to be found and returned to his family."

"He doesn't have a family. He was in foster care." Johnny stood up a little straighter in defense of Sawyer.

"I'm sorry about that, but that doesn't change the rules."

He focused his attention on their father again. "I take it you didn't know anything about this?"

Their *daed* shook his head slowly, his mouth pressed into a grim line.

"Okay, here's what we'll do. The fire's out, so our work is done here. I'll try to find out who owns the property. There wasn't any residual damage to the field or the trees nearby, so that's a good thing. But I will notify the police. You should be hearing from them sometime tomorrow. They'll look for Sawyer. If you hear from him, make sure to notify them immediately." He held out his hand to their father but looked at Mary Beth and Johnny as he spoke. "We'll be in touch."

Mary Beth shivered. The rain had stopped, and the air had cooled down tremendously. But she wasn't cold. She was afraid. Like the firefighter, she chose to believe Sawyer was out there. But if he was caught, he'd go back to foster care, the one thing he feared the most. She was also afraid for herself and Johnny. If she had thought her father was angry when he'd found them at the barn, he was fuming mad right now, even though he displayed no emotion. But that was how she could tell. He was stone-faced and wouldn't even look at them. *"Kinder,"* he said, turning around and walking toward their house. "Come with me. *Now.*"

Mary Beth started to follow their father when she heard Johnny whistle. "C'mon, *bu,*" he said.

She turned around, expecting to find the dog right beside Johnny. But he wasn't. She looked around the field, at the smoldering barn, even toward the road. But the dog wasn't anywhere in sight. "Roscoe?"

"*Kinder!*"

Johnny and Mary Beth both trotted up to their father, not wanting to make him angrier than he already was. They'd worry about Roscoe later. Right now they had to worry about themselves.

They didn't say anything for a long time, just kept following their father. Mary Beth slipped on the wet grass but maintained her balance. Johnny came up beside her, his hands shoved in his pockets, his chin nearly touching his chest.

"*Daed* is really mad," he said. "I've never seen him so mad."

"I know." Mary Beth trudged through the soggy grass, still keeping her arms crossed. A short while ago it had been so hot; now she was shivering.

"He's going to ground us until we're forty."

"I don't care." She looked at him. "How can you be thinking about us when Sawyer's out there somewhere?"

"You think I don't know that?" Johnny scowled. "But there's nothing we can do for him. Not anymore. Not after tonight."

When they reached the house, *Daed* walked inside first, not waiting for Johnny or Mary Beth. They stepped into the kitchen, the hem of Mary Beth's nightgown still dripping wet. She stayed in the doorway, with Johnny right behind her. He must have had the same thought. Why make things worse by dripping water on the kitchen floor?

Their *daed* finally turned around, oblivious to the fact that he was dripping on the floor. "Dry off, change your clothes, and go to bed." With that he turned around and went upstairs.

Johnny and Mary Beth looked at each other. Even though their father hadn't yelled at them or grounded them, Mary Beth still knew they were in trouble. Now they had the rest of the night to imagine their punishment.

And Sawyer was missing.

Eleven

AFTER A sleepless night, Mary Beth got up before the sun and headed downstairs. Without waiting for her mother to ask, she went outside and got the eggs. She planned to have breakfast ready so neither of her parents had to do any of the work. Besides, she couldn't stay in bed any longer, worrying about Sawyer. As she passed the barn, she heard the pigs oinking and squealing. Thinking they might still be out of sorts from the storm last night, she went inside the barn. She was surprised to see Johnny there, dumping feed into their trough.

"You're up early." She tucked the bowl of eggs into the crook of her arm.

"You too."

"Thought I'd make breakfast for everyone," she said.

"And I thought I'd get this done before *Daed* had to say anything." He dropped the empty bucket next to the pen and walked over to Mary Beth. His hair was standing up all over his head, even more so than usual, a reminder of what had happened last night. Like her, he'd probably run a towel through it and gone straight to bed. At least this morning she had taken time to comb her hair and put it up, putting on her black *kapp* and making extra sure it was on straight. She'd put on a fresh dress too. She didn't want to do anything else to aggravate her parents.

"What do you think they're gonna do to us?" Johnny said, running a hand through his messy hair. The gesture only served to make it more unruly.

She shook her head. "I have no idea." Numerous scenarios had gone through her mind last night, from being grounded to the house for the rest of the summer to being forbidden from seeing their friends for months. Surely extra chores would be involved. If word got out to the community about what they'd done, her parents would be embarrassed. *What a mess.*

Johnny blew out a breath. "We better get back inside before they wake up. If *Daed* finds us out here, he might think we're up to something. I don't want to make him any angrier."

"I'm not sure that's possible. He's really steamed right now."

As they went inside, Johnny asked, "What do you think happened to Sawyer?"

"I don't know. Maybe he made good on his threat to leave. I hope he did, because that would mean for sure he wasn't in the barn."

"But where could he have gone?"

She shrugged. That was a mystery, one they would probably never solve. If Sawyer was gone, and she prayed he was, she would never see him again. Frankly, she'd had enough of mysteries for a while.

When they reached the back deck, she looked at her brother. "If you had to do it all over again, would you?"

"You mean help out Sawyer?"

She nodded.

He rubbed his nose but didn't reply right away. Finally he responded. "*Ya*. What about you?"

"Definitely."

They walked back in the house, and the first thing Mary Beth noticed was that the light was on. Someone was up, but the kitchen was empty. She hurried to set the eggs on the counter, washed her hands, then started breakfast. By the time she got the bacon cooking and the eggs scrambled, her mother had come into the kitchen.

"*Guten morgen*," Mary Beth said tentatively.

Her mother looked at her briefly, then went to the pantry. "*Guten morgen*." Her tone sounded grim.

Mary Beth's heart sank. She finished making the rest of breakfast in awkward silence. Her mother had put a loaf of bread and butter on the table and poured milk for everyone but their father, who preferred coffee. When he came in and sat down at the table, Mary Beth filled up his mug, added a splash of milk, and took it to him.

"*Guten morgen, Daed*." She handed him the mug, trying to be as pleasant as she possibly could.

He took it from her but didn't say anything. *Mami* went to get Micah just as Johnny and Caleb walked in. "Pigs are done," Johnny said, sitting next to *Daed*.

He nodded, slowly sipping his coffee but not really acknowledging Johnny. Mary Beth put the rest of the breakfast on the table as *Mami* sat Micah in his chair. The family bowed their heads and prayed, but not a word was uttered during the meal. Even Micah and Caleb were quiet, as if they knew something was wrong.

Daed wiped his mouth and stood up from the table. "Mary Beth, come help me hitch up the buggy."

Mary Beth's head shot up from her barely eaten meal. "What?"

"I want you to come outside and help me with the buggy," he said, his face emotionless. Then he turned around and walked out the door.

She looked at her *mami*, who gave her a curt nod then rose and started clearing the dishes. When Mary Beth moved to help, *Mami* said, "Your father asked you to do something. You'd better go do it."

Nodding, she set her plate down and ran out the door. When she reached the barn, her father was already leading Crackerjack out of his stall.

As Mary Beth helped him hook up the buggy to Crackerjack, she couldn't stand the silence stretching out between them. Her father had never asked her to help with this chore; usually he relied on one of her brothers. There must be a reason he wanted her out here with him.

Once the horse was hitched up, her father climbed into the buggy, using his good arm to hoist himself in. He reached for the reins, and Mary Beth thought he would leave without saying anything to her. Then he spoke.

"Tell me the truth, Mary Beth. What you were saying last night about that boy . . . did Johnny put you up to it?"

She shook her head. *"Nee, Daed.* He didn't."

"Are you sure? Or are you just trying to protect him?"

Mary Beth thought about all the times Johnny had annoyed her. The tricks he'd played on her, like scaring her in the barn a few weeks ago, so much that she'd landed on her rear end. How he had gone in her room without permission. Even the fact that he said he would have read her journal proved how little respect he had for her. Now she had the opportunity to get herself out of trouble. She could blame all this on Johnny, and her father would believe it. She had the chance to get back at him for all the times he had made her mad. Even if Johnny tried to defend himself, her father would believe her over him. She was the trustworthy one, the one who never got in trouble, who always did as she was told.

Yet she was far from perfect. She had kept her own secret about the barn, long before Johnny ever found out. It was her fault all this had started in the first place. And even if that wasn't the case, she couldn't bring herself to let Johnny take all the blame. It wouldn't be honest, and it wouldn't be right. "Johnny didn't make me do anything, *Daed.* This was all my fault."

Her father looked surprised. "I find that hard to believe."

"It's true." She looked down at the ground, ashamed.

Crackerjack whinnied, and her father tugged on his reins. "We'll have a long talk about this when I get home tonight. Me, you, Johnny, and your mother. In the meantime, I want to make something perfectly clear. Do not, under any circumstances, go to that old barn. You are not to leave the house today, unless your *mami* asks you to do something outside for her. Understood?"

Mary Beth nodded, taking a few steps back from the buggy. Her father tapped the reins on the black horse's flanks and steered the buggy down the driveway and onto the road.

She watched until her father disappeared into the distance, pressing her top teeth down on her lower lip. When he was gone, she turned to see Johnny heading toward her, a worried look on his face.

"What did *Daed* say?" he asked.

She paused, ready to tell him that their father thought he was to blame for all this. But she changed her mind. Johnny didn't need to know that, especially since it wasn't true. She'd make sure her father understood that completely when he came home tonight. "He told me to stay in the house," she said, brushing past him and heading toward the back porch.

"That's all?"

"He also said he and *Mami* will be having a long talk with us tonight."

"Finally. It's about time." Johnny hopped up the back deck steps. "This silent treatment drives me crazy. I wish they would just yell at us or something. I can't stand the silence. It just piles on the guilt. And I'm feeling guilty enough already." He walked inside, the door shutting behind him.

Mary Beth sighed. She knew exactly what he meant.

"The police came by work today," *Daed* said as he sat down on the couch. His injured hand lay limply against his side. Caleb and Micah were already upstairs in bed. A single gas lamp sat in the corner, attached to a long pole connected to a propane tank, casting a yellowish light in the room. The lamp hissed, filling the quiet in the room.

Mary Beth swallowed and looked at Johnny. He seemed pale. He was sitting on his hands in a hardback chair across from the couch. He turned from Mary Beth and stared at his lap.

"What did they say?" Mary Beth asked.

"They wanted to know more about Sawyer. I told them I had no idea who they were talking about, other than what you two said about him last night. The police then said they wanted to talk to you, but I told them they couldn't, not until I knew what was going on. They'll be back tomorrow morning." He leaned forward and looked first at Mary Beth, then at Johnny. "Now, start from the beginning. And don't leave anything out."

Mary Beth and Johnny took turns telling their parents about what had happened during the past month. When Mary Beth admitted she'd been sneaking out to the barn since early spring, her mother's disappointed look nearly crushed her. She remembered her mother telling her how important it was that she could put her trust in Mary Beth. Now she wondered if her parents would ever trust her again.

Her father glared at her. "You went out there even though we told you not to?"

She nodded, her face heating up. "I'm sorry. But I wanted to have some privacy."

"You have a bedroom."

She tried to explain, hoping they would understand. "The boys wouldn't leave me alone. They were always coming inside uninvited. They'd mess with my stuff. I just wanted a place where I didn't have to worry about them bugging me."

"And you thought that was more important than your parents' wishes?"

She glanced down. "*Ya*. I know it was wrong, and I'm sorry. It won't ever happen again."

Her father's face grew red. "*Nee*, it won't, and not only because the barn burned down. Mary Beth, that barn was a very dangerous place. There was a reason we had forbidden you and your brothers from going over there. The wood was rotted. It could have easily collapsed on you, and we might not have known about it until it was too late. And you saw how easily it caught on fire. What if *you* had been in there?" He clenched his fist. "How could you disobey us like this? When your *mami* and I tell you not to do something, we expect you to do what you're told!"

Mary Beth looked at her mother. The disappointment was still evident in her eyes, but they had softened. Her mother understood her need to be alone. She'd had brothers, and she knew what it was like. That didn't make what Mary Beth had done right, and she knew that, but knowing her mother comprehended the reasons for her disobedience was a comfort.

Her *daed* took a breath and looked at Johnny, this time his tone less harsh. "When did you get involved in all this?"

"I followed Mary Beth out there one day. She'd gotten mad and left one day, and I wanted to find out where she was going. Then I saw her enter the old barn." He proceeded to finish the story, telling their parents how they eventually discovered Sawyer.

"Why didn't you tell us about this before?" their mother asked.

"Because Sawyer made us promise not to," Mary Beth answered. "He said if we told anyone, he would run away."

"We didn't want him to do that, because we knew he didn't have anyplace else to go. At least he had a place to stay in the barn. So we kept his secret."

"And we snuck food to him when we could. He was really hungry when we found him."

Their parents looked at each other. "That explains the disappearing peanut butter," *Mami* said. "And why we have had fewer leftovers than before." She looked at Johnny. "So you weren't sneaking midnight snacks?"

He shook his head. "Not that I haven't been tempted. But *nee*, whatever you noticed missing was the food we took out to Sawyer."

Mami wrinkled her brow. "How did you get the food to him?"

Mary Beth crossed her feet at the ankles. "We put a box by the pond and put the food in it. He would pick it up. That way we didn't have to sneak out in the middle of the night."

"You were sneaking out at *night?*" *Daed* sounded upset and shocked at the same time.

"Um, *ya*." This was getting worse by the minute, but they had to reveal everything. "But only a couple of times."

"We stopped doing it once we put the box out by the pond," Johnny added. "We didn't want to sneak out anymore."

"You don't seem to have a problem doing it during the day," *Mami* said, frowning.

Guilt flowed over her. "We wanted to help him, *Mami*. We didn't know what else to do."

Mami sat back in her chair and looked at *Daed*, shaking her head. "I don't know whether to be proud of them or angry with them."

Daed nodded, looking much less furious than before. "I'll admit, I'm a little of both."

Mary Beth's mouth dropped open. She looked at Johnny, who seemed equally as shocked. Her parents were proud of them? How was that possible? "We broke the rules," Mary Beth said, not understanding.

"*Ya*, you did," *Daed* said. "And that was wrong. But trying to help someone when he was in need was right. You just went about it the wrong way. How old is Sawyer?"

"Our age, I think," Mary Beth said.

"He's fourteen," Johnny said. He looked at Mary Beth. "He told me that the other day."

"He's young. Too young to know what's best for him. He had no right to make you promise to keep his secret. You should have come and told us about him right away."

Johnny moved to the edge of his chair. "But *Daed*, his parents just died not too long ago. You should have heard what happened to him in foster care. They beat him! I don't blame him for running away. Or for being afraid that he might get sent back."

"I know you don't, Johnny."

"So you see why we couldn't tell you?"

"Believe me, *sohn*, I do see. But how did running away solve the problem? As you found out, it didn't. It only created new ones. Do you have any idea where he is now?"

They both shook their head. "He and I got into a fight yesterday," Mary Beth said.

Mami frowned. "You were at the barn on the Lord's day?"

"*Nee*. He met me at the pond. I didn't even know he was coming. He just showed up. We fought because he . . ." She entwined her fingers together. Looking back, she knew now that the reason they had gotten into the fight was a foolish one. She didn't want to admit this, but she needed to be honest about everything with her parents. Dishonesty had gotten them into this mess. "He read my journal and I got mad. Then he told me he was leaving."

"He could be long gone by now," Johnny said, sounding worried.

Daed rubbed his beard. "I doubt it. With the storm last night, he couldn't have gotten very far." He stood up. "I'll go next door and call the police and tell them what happened."

Mary Beth jumped up from her seat. "You can't!"

"I have to. They need to know what's been going on so they can find him."

"Will they take him back to the foster home?" she asked, saying a silent prayer that her father would say no.

Daed looked down at her, sorrow in his eyes. "Probably."

Johnny joined them. "He won't go. He said that a hundred times, and I believe him."

"He'll have to. The police will make him." *Daed* sighed. "I'm sorry, but there's nothing else we can do for him. We can't keep hiding him; that's illegal."

"But who has to know he's here? We don't have to say anything to them. They'll never find out he's missing."

"Mary Beth, they already know he's missing, thanks to the barn burning up. They're not going to stop searching for him until they find him. Besides, he doesn't have a place to stay or food to eat. That's no way for a young boy to live."

"I know he can't live like that permanently. So maybe he could live here? With us?"

"Mary Beth," her mother said, sounding shocked at the idea.

Johnny jumped up from his chair, his eyes lighting up with enthusiasm. "He could bunk in with me and Caleb. We don't mind."

Daed frowned. "You're speaking for Caleb now?"

"And I would share my food with him," Mary Beth added, too excited to realize what her father had just said.

"Me too," Johnny added. "We're used to it anyway."

"And he could help with the chores."

"He already helped me clean out the chicken coop. Did a *gut* job, too, except for the times he threw the stinky hay on me. But he didn't know how to do it right, so I didn't get too mad."

"See, it will work out perfectly." Mary Beth looked at her father, then to her mother. "Please?"

Her *daed* gave her a half smile, then touched her cheek. "I'm sorry. We can't afford another mouth to feed, especially with the *boppli* coming."

"But you always say the Lord will provide. If we do what's right, he'll make sure we have enough."

"Oh, Mary Beth. If only everyone had the faith you have. And it's true, God provides. But he also asks us to make wise choices. We simply can't afford for him to stay here. I'm sorry. I wish it could be different, I really do. Johnny, come with me next door." He picked up his hat off the coffee table and both of them left the living room, Johnny dragging behind him.

Mary Beth plopped down on the chair, her throat burning, barely able to stand the disappointment. How could her father say no so quickly? He hadn't even thought about the situation, or tried to come up with a different solution. He just went to call the police, who would find Sawyer and take him back to that horrible place. "He'll just run away again," she muttered, crossing her arms.

"You're right, he just might do that." *Mami* rose from her chair and moved to the couch. She patted the space next to her. "Mary Beth, come here."

Mary Beth went to her mother and sat down, making sure there was space between them, still afraid her mother might be angry. She couldn't believe her parents were acting so calmly about this. They had raised their voices a couple of times, and considering the circumstances, that was understandable. But neither of them had mentioned punishment. So she kept her guard up. She knew she wouldn't get out of this scot-free.

"I'm not going to condone what you and Johnny did," *Mami* said, looking at her.

"What does *condone* mean?"

"It means to say what you did was okay. I can't do that, because it was wrong. But I understand why you did it." Her eyes misted over. "I'm amazed you would risk getting into trouble for a stranger."

"But we're supposed to help people if we can. You and *Daed* taught us that."

Mami reached for Mary Beth's hand and gave it a squeeze. "I'm glad to see you learned the lesson. And that you do listen to us sometimes."

Feeling a little bit better, Mary Beth scooted closer to her mother. "I'm worried about Sawyer. I thought he might have been in the barn when the fire broke out, but he wasn't. I don't know where he is."

"Does he have any money?"

Shaking her head, Mary Beth said, *"Nee."*

"And he said he didn't have any family?"

"No one. His parents were the only family he had. And then they died and he was in a group home. After that he went to a couple of foster families. He said this last one was really mean."

"That's very sad." *Mami* wiped underneath her eyes with her fingertips.

"So you see why he doesn't want to go back? I wouldn't want to go back there either."

"I understand, Mary Beth. It seems like a horrible situation. But like your father said, he doesn't have anywhere to go, and we can't let him stay here."

"What if he lived with someone else? Is there anyone else in the church who might take him in?"

Her mother paused. "I'm not sure, Mary Beth. It's a complicated situation. He's a Yankee, and he's already been placed with a family. I don't know what the rules are for foster care, but I don't think we can get involved in this. It's better for the police to handle it."

"Better for who?"

Her mother sighed and put her arm around Mary Beth's shoulders, drawing her close. "I don't know," she said sadly. "I really don't know."

Mary Beth closed her eyes and leaned against her mother. She didn't know either. All she could do was hope and pray that Sawyer would be all right.

Sawyer stood by the ashes of the old barn. He stuck his toe into the grayish black pile that used to be the front wall of the structure. The barn hadn't burned completely to the ground, but it was a charred shell of what it had been. Which wasn't saying much, considering the bad shape it had been in before the fire.

He shoved his hands into the pockets of his damp jeans. The storm last night had hit just as he had made his way into the middle of the woods. With the lightning striking all around him and thunder scaring him almost out of his mind, he had crouched underneath a tree and waited out the storm. It was now dusk, and it had taken him that long to gather the courage to come out of hiding. Not because of the storm, but because of the sirens he'd heard. He had smelled the smoke and thought the barn was on fire. When he had emerged from the woods, it made him sad to see it was true.

He assumed the sirens he heard were fire trucks, but they could have been police too. He thought he'd heard Mary Beth call his name, but he wasn't sure. He doubted she would have been out in the storm last night. But he was sure she knew about the fire. She was probably devastated that her secret place was now a pile of burnt wood and ash.

He certainly was.

Sighing, he knelt down and picked up some ashes, letting them sift through his fingers. Some of them disappeared into the air in a puff of dusty smoke; the rest of them fell to the ground. Why was he still here? The storm had ended last night. There was no reason not to be on his way. Now that the fire department knew about the barn, it would be only a matter of time before Mary Beth and Johnny said something about him. If they hadn't already.

He stood up and slapped his palms against each other, removing the ash residue from his skin. He suddenly heard the sound of a car coming near, and he saw a police cruiser driving over the grass and heading toward the barn.

Time to go.

He started to run, spinning on his heel. But his ankle suddenly twisted in the still slippery grass, and he fell to the ground. Pain shot through his leg. When he tried to get up, he could barely stand on his foot. He heard a car door slam. They were coming.

Grinding his teeth against the pain, he fled into the woods and hid behind a thick tree that had fallen to the ground. He lay against it, stretching out his body, his ankle throbbing. He listened for footsteps coming closer, the crunch of boots on the leaves as they searched for him among the dense trees. He held his breath, waiting for them to find him. For the first time in his life, he closed his eyes and prayed. *Please don't let them find me!*

A minute passed. Then a few more. It took awhile, but

he finally realized no one was coming. Just to make sure, he poked his head above the log. He didn't see or hear anyone.

He let out a long sigh of relief, then started to move. He winced at the pain in his ankle. It felt like someone was stabbing it with a knife. He sat up, then yanked up his pant leg. His ankle had already started to swell.

Great. Just great.

Gingerly he rose, testing his foot and ankle to see if he could stand up. He could if he was on his tiptoes, but he had to bite his cheek with every step he took. Limping, he searched around the woods, trying to find some kind of stick he could use for a cane. His gaze latched onto a gnarled, crooked tree branch. He picked it up. It would work. At least it would get him out of the woods.

But then what? He wouldn't get very far with his ankle like this. What if it was broken? Leave it to him to do something stupid to screw everything up. Now he didn't even have the barn to go back to. The fire wasn't his fault; it must have been struck by lightning last night. But he still couldn't believe his bad luck. He had to find help, and he knew of only one place where he would get it. At least he hoped. After what he'd said to Mary Beth the last time he saw her, he wouldn't be surprised if she turned him away.

He looked around, making sure no one was watching him. Satisfied he was alone, he reluctantly made his way across the field to Mary Beth and Johnny's house.

Twelve

THAT NIGHT Mary Beth had gone to bed early. After everything that had happened and a night of no sleep, she was exhausted. Her father had returned with Johnny a couple of hours earlier. They had called the police, who had asked their *daed* a few questions, then wanted to talk to Johnny. When they had come back home, Johnny didn't say anything, just headed upstairs to his room. Their *daed* had said they would discuss the consequences in the morning and also retired for the night.

Mary Beth lay in bed, and despite her tiredness, she couldn't fall asleep. Her mind kept reliving everything that had happened. Although she tried, she couldn't stop wondering where Sawyer was.

She rolled over on her side, closing her eyes tight, willing herself to fall asleep. Just as she had found a comfortable position, she heard the door to her room open. Startled, she bolted upright in bed. "Who's there?"

Johnny whispered, "It's me," and padded over to her bed. "Sawyer's outside."

"What?"

"Not so loud. You're gonna wake up *Mami* and *Daed*."

She lowered her voice. "How do you know he's outside?"

"I couldn't sleep, so I was counting stars—"

"You snuck outside *again*? What were you thinking?"

"Shh. Are you *ab im kopp*? Keep your voice down."

"Sorry."

Johnny continued. "*Nee*, I didn't sneak outside. I was sitting by the window. You think I'm stupid enough to go outside?" He shrugged. "Anyway, I heard a noise outside and I looked down and he was underneath my window. He's limping, and he's using a stick to walk."

"He's hurt?"

Johnny nodded.

"Did you say anything to him?"

"I told him to hang on, then I came in here. What are we gonna do? If we tell *Mami* and *Daed*, he's just going to run off again."

"If he's hurt, he won't get very far."

"He'll still try. He's got to know about the barn by now. What I don't understand is why he came back here."

"He came back because he needs our help." She climbed out of bed. "I'll go let him inside."

"Mary Beth—"

"And you go wake up *Mami* and *Daed*. Maybe if they meet Sawyer, they'll change their minds about letting him stay here."

"I doubt it."

Mary Beth glared at him.

"Okay, okay, I'm going."

Johnny disappeared to wake their parents while Mary Beth slipped out of her room. She went downstairs and opened the back door. She saw Sawyer standing near the house. Like Johnny had said, he was holding a stick. His left leg was bent at the knee, his foot off the ground.

"Sawyer," she said, whispering his name loudly. "Come here." She motioned toward him with her arm.

He hesitated a moment before limping to her. She met him at the bottom of the steps. "Come inside," she said, putting her hand on his arm. "I'll help you up the stairs."

He shook his head. "I can't."

"Why not?"

"Your parents will wake up and find me here." He looked up at her. She couldn't see his face in the dark, but she could sense his fear. "Do they know about me?"

She ignored his question, unwilling to lie to him. She'd been lying enough as it was. "You're hurt. Come inside and I can help you."

"No."

Exasperated, she put her hands on her hips. "Then why are you here?"

He slumped and leaned against the stick. "I don't know."

"I do. Now let me help you inside. We'll figure out what to do once you're sitting down."

He finally agreed, and she helped him get up the stairs. She led him into the kitchen, to the chair nearest to the sink.

She went to the counter and turned on the light her parents kept there. She blinked against the brightness, then turned around. He was sitting in the chair, staring straight ahead. She went over to him, took the stick from his hand, and laid it against the wall. This time he didn't protest.

"How did you hurt yourself?"

"Tripped over my own two feet." He looked up at her. "Dumb, wasn't it?"

She shook her head. "I've done that before, so I guess that makes me dumb too. Let me take a look at it."

He lifted it up and propped it on the chair. He had rolled his pant leg up, revealing his swollen, black-and-blue ankle. He had on his old, sad-looking tennis shoes and no socks. It struck her at that moment that she missed seeing him in Amish clothes. Somehow he had looked right in them.

"Now what?" he said, sounding tired.

"I can put a cold cloth on it. That's what *Mami* does sometimes when we're hurt. But other than that, I don't know." She looked at him. "You need to see a doctor."

"Oh no." He put his foot down on the floor and moved to get up. "I'm not seeing no doctor."

"You will if you have to." *Daed* suddenly entered the kitchen, wearing a white T-shirt and dark blue pants. Johnny and their mother followed close behind.

Sawyer looked at Mary Beth, betrayal in his eyes. "You snitched on me," he said.

She started to speak when Johnny moved in front of her.

"No, she didn't," he said. "I did. And I'm not sorry about it, either."

Mami went to Sawyer and looked at his ankle. Instead of her usual white *kapp*, she had a light blue kerchief on her head, but she had put on her work dress before coming to the kitchen. She turned to *Daed*. "It's pretty swollen, Daniel. I think it's sprained."

Daed rubbed his bearded chin. "Johnny," he said, "go downstairs and get some ice cubes. Mary Beth, get a towel to put them in. The ice will help with swelling."

"Don't bother. I don't need this," Sawyer said, moving to stand up again. "I'm getting out of here."

Daed calmly put his hand on Sawyer's shoulder. "Wrong. What you're going to do is sit and listen. Understand?"

Sawyer looked at the man's hand on his shoulder. He was tempted to shrug it off, but his grip, which was gentle yet firm, held him still. If he tried to leave, he wouldn't get very far. Thanks to Johnny and Mary Beth, he had no choice but to stay. "Fine," Sawyer said. "I'll listen. Then I'm gone."

He heard Johnny scrambling up the stairs behind him. "Got the ice cubes."

Mary Beth held out a small white towel and Johnny dumped them there. She wrapped the towel around the ice cubes and handed it to her mother. Mrs. Mullet balanced the ice pack on his ankle, then stepped away from him.

"Seems like you're in a bit of trouble," Mr. Mullet said, looking down at him.

Sawyer didn't answer. Obviously Johnny had told them everything. *Traitor.* From the guilty look on Mary Beth's face, he figured she'd also added her two cents. He crossed his arms over his chest, staring at his ankle, refusing to look at any of them.

"The police are looking for you," Mr. Mullet continued.

Silence.

"They've been in touch with social services in Lake County, where your foster family is. They reported you missing last week."

Figures. He'd actually been gone for a month. He refused to let them know that and stayed silent.

"Hear you've been living in the barn for a while. Must have been hard on you."

Sawyer sat still.

"How did you get way over here to Middlefield?"

They'd have to torture him to get him to reveal any information. When he was younger he'd watched a few spy movies with his father. He knew how interrogation worked. If they thought he would break that easily, they had another thing coming.

Mr. Mullet pulled out a chair and sat down across the table from him. "We want to help you, *sohn*. But we can't if you won't talk to us."

Against his will, he looked at Johnny and Mary Beth's *daed*. "I've heard that before. I don't need your kind of help."

"But you didn't have a problem taking it from my *kinder*?"

"That's different. They were only giving me food and stuff."

Mr. Mullet smiled. "Only."

Guilt shot through Sawyer's defenses, but he ignored it. He turned from Mr. Mullet and went back to staring at his leg again.

"Sawyer, why are you here?" Mr. Mullet asked.

"What do you mean?"

"Why even come here if you didn't need us?" When Sawyer didn't answer, Mr. Mullet added, "I think you came here because you're tired of running. You know you don't have anywhere else to go."

Sawyer fought back the lump forming in his throat. He couldn't show emotion around these people. Even though the ice they gave him was helping his ankle. And being in the kitchen reminded him of the delicious meal Mary Beth had made for him awhile back. He'd do anything to have another meal like that again. Anything except tell them what they wanted to know. He especially couldn't let the kindness he saw in Mrs. Mullet's eyes and the understanding he heard in Mr. Mullet's voice affect him. It was a trick. The only thing saving him from being escorted out by the police right now was the fact that they didn't have a phone.

"He's not going to tell you anything." Mrs. Mullet stood up. She lifted the ice pack and checked his ankle, then set it back down. "At least not tonight."

Mr. Mullet frowned, tugging on his beard again. He

didn't have a mustache, which Sawyer thought was strange. Not that it mattered to him whether or not Mr. Mullet wore a mustache. But he had a fleeting thought that it might be a part of the dress code these people followed.

"Why don't we talk about this in the morning? It's too late to do anything tonight." She looked directly at Sawyer, and just like her husband, kindness shone in her eyes. "Are you hungry?"

He shook his head, but it was difficult for him to deny the truth. He was starving. He hadn't eaten for almost two days. He'd been so thirsty he broke down and drank some of the pond water, amazed that it didn't make him sick. But he wasn't about to admit any of that, either.

Mrs. Mullet didn't say anything else to him. Instead she walked over to the pantry and pulled out a loaf of bread, a jar of peanut butter, and a small jar of homemade jam. She gave the ingredients to Mary Beth, who turned around and started making a sandwich without being asked. Johnny had already run downstairs again. For what, Sawyer had no idea. But the scent of peanut butter made his stomach growl with hunger.

Within a few moments there was a fresh peanut-butter-and-jelly sandwich and a cold glass of milk on the table in front of him. Just looking at the soft bread made his mouth water. Still, he didn't reach for the food. He didn't want them to know how desperate he was.

"Don't be so stubborn," Mary Beth said, moving to stand by him. She smiled. "We can tell you're hungry. Just eat."

Unable to resist, Sawyer shoved almost half the sandwich in his mouth, then washed it down with the milk. He had the sandwich polished off in record time. Having something in his stomach made him feel a lot better. Even though he didn't want to, he couldn't stop himself from saying, "Thank you."

"You're welcome." Mr. Mullet stood up and stretched. "We need to get to bed. We can sort this out in the morning. Johnny, you and Sawyer can bunk out in the living room."

"Wait," Sawyer said. "I can't stay here."

"Oh? You have somewhere else you need to be?"

Sawyer paused, then shook his head.

"You take the couch; Johnny will sleep on the floor."

"Now wait a minute. I'll sleep on the floor."

"*Nee*," Johnny said. "I'm sleeping on the floor."

"No, I'm sleeping—"

"Enough!" Mr. Mullet's voice echoed in the room. "Johnny will take the floor, you'll take the couch, and there'll be no more arguments. Got it?"

Sawyer and Johnny both nodded and kept their mouths shut.

A short while later Sawyer was lying on the couch, his body sinking into the soft cushions. He had a fluffy pillow underneath his head and a clean-smelling quilt nearby in case he needed a cover. Johnny had loaned him clothes again, and Sawyer could tell that these weren't old ones. He didn't even know what happened to his other clothes. At that moment he didn't care.

Johnny had made a pallet on the floor while his parents

and Mary Beth went upstairs. She had lingered on the bottom stair and looked at him. He couldn't read her expression. Then she suddenly dashed up the stairs.

The house was dark and very, very quiet. Almost too quiet. At his foster home there was always the blare of the TV in the background, even at night. And while he had been living outside, the sounds of the crickets and frogs had put him to sleep. But this house was silent, except for the sound of Johnny's faint snoring.

Sawyer shifted on the couch, wincing at the stab of pain in his ankle. His ankle felt better than it did before, but it still ached. The longer he lay there, the more he thought about getting up and leaving, but he couldn't exactly make a good getaway with a gimp leg. He also couldn't bring himself to do that, especially after all the Mullets had done for him so far.

Suddenly he could barely keep his eyes open. Even with his pain and worry, he still felt more comfortable than he had in weeks. His eyelids closing, he fell into a deep, welcome sleep.

From her bedroom, Mary Beth could hear the murmur of her parents' voices. She couldn't make out what they were saying, but she knew they had to be talking about Sawyer. Her curiosity getting the best of her, she left her room and crept down the hall, crouching down in front of their bedroom. She put her ear to the door.

"He seems like a nice boy, Daniel," *Mami* said. "A little lost, but after what he's been through, you can't blame him. I don't see why he can't stay here with us, at least for a little while."

"Hannah, you know it's not possible. Even if we could convince the foster care people he'd be okay here, we can't afford it. Not with the *boppli* coming."

"But shouldn't we have faith that God will provide? Mary Beth and Johnny believe that. I think we can learn a lesson from our children about that."

Mary Beth heard her father sigh. "I know, Hannah. And I know God provides. Look how he has taken care of us since my accident. I thought I'd lose my job at the buggy shop, but the Yoders kept me on, even though I can't do the work as fast as I used to before. But that still doesn't mean we're going to have enough money to take in another child. And I don't want you taking on more jobs than you have. You work too hard. I feel guilty enough about that."

"I don't mind the work, Daniel. I'm sure I can find a couple more people I can sew for—"

"I'm not changing my mind about that, Hannah. You're not to take in any more work."

"But . . ." After a long pause she spoke again. "All right. I won't. Regardless, I think we should seriously consider giving that boy a home."

"Hannah—"

"Let me finish. It's not like we're talking about a *boppli*, or even a young child. You saw him. He's thin and weak now, but once he gets food in him, he'll be strong. He can find work. At the very least he'll be able to help out around here."

"Our own *kinder* do a good enough job of that. You know if we take this boy in and put him to work, the Yankees will just take him away. They'll think we wanted him just so we could have an extra pair of hands around here."

"Daniel!" Her mother sounded horrified. "I didn't mean . . . Of course we wouldn't do that. I just—"

"I know." *Daed*'s voice softened, and Mary Beth could hear footsteps in the room. They started talking again in hushed tones, making it harder for her to hear. She pressed her ear harder against the door.

"You're letting me know he's not going to be a burden," *Daed* said. "Hannah, I would like nothing better than to give that boy a home. If Mary Beth and Johnny were willing to get in trouble to help him, he must be special. But we can't."

Mary Beth thought she heard her mother sniff. "Daniel—"

"I mean it, Hannah." He didn't raise his voice, but from his tone, Mary Beth knew her mother wasn't going to argue the point further. Mary Beth bit her bottom lip, trying to stem her disappointment.

"Is there anyone else who might be able to take him in?" *Mami* asked. "What about Lukas and Anna Byler?"

"Moriah's brother and his wife?"

"*Ya*. It's a sad thing, but you know they can't have children."

"They're *also* newly married. I'd be surprised if they'd agree to take in a child now, much less a Yankee teenager."

"But it's worth a try, don't you think?"

"Hannah, I don't know . . . Maybe we should just mind our own business. Lukas might not appreciate me asking him for such a thing."

"How will you know if you don't try? Please, Daniel, just speak to him. Explain what happened, and tell him he doesn't have to feel obligated. But at least give him the choice."

"And if he says *nee*?"

"Then we'll have to accept that."

Mary Beth held her breath as she waited for her father to make up his mind. She squeezed her eyes shut and prayed he would say yes, and if he did, that Mr. Byler would agree to take Sawyer. After what seemed like forever, her father finally gave *Mami* his answer.

"All right. I'll ask him. But we have to call the police first thing in the morning. We need to get things straightened out with the Yankees and make sure it's okay for me to even bring it up to Lukas."

Mary Beth grinned. She wanted to run downstairs and tell Sawyer the good news. He might be able to live in Middlefield.

"We also have to be prepared for Sawyer to say no," *Daed* added. "He might not want to live among us. He's only known Yankee ways all his life. It would be difficult for him to give up what he's been used to, especially worldly things."

"That may be the case, but he should at least have the chance to choose. You heard what Mary Beth and Johnny said. That boy's lost so much already."

Her parents talked for a little while longer; then she saw the light underneath their door go out. She tiptoed back to her room and climbed in bed, excited. She couldn't wait to tell Sawyer the news. He'd be even more excited than she was. She didn't know how she'd be able to fall asleep, but after a long time, she did.

The next morning she woke up just as the sun pinked the sky. The rooster crowed several times, signaling the start of the day. Mary Beth jumped out of bed and quickly dressed, hastily pinning a kerchief to her head instead of wearing her *kapp*. She flew downstairs, ready to deliver the good news to Sawyer. He might have a home here in Middlefield after all. He wouldn't have to go back to foster care. She could imagine how excited he would be to hear that.

But when she reached the living room, he was gone.

She drew in a deep breath, unable to believe what she was seeing. He'd run away again. She should have known he wouldn't stay.

But how far could he get on a sprained foot? And what if he injured himself even more?

Frustrated, she looked at her brother, who was sleeping soundly on the floor. She went over to him and woke him up. "Johnny! Where's Sawyer?"

"What?" His eyes opened to slits.

"Sawyer. He's gone!" She stood and pointed to the empty couch. "How could you let him run away again?"

"Me?" Johnny sat up. "I was sleeping. I didn't hear a thing."

"You should have kept watch."

"Oh yeah? Why didn't you keep watch?"

"You were down here."

"Excuse me for sleeping."

"What on earth is going on here?" *Mami* came downstairs, stopping at the last step. "You two could wake the whole town with your arguing."

Mary Beth ran over to her. "Sawyer's gone."

Mami's face turned white. "He is? When?"

"I don't know. Johnny let him go."

"I did not." He scrambled up from the floor. "I was asleep. He must have snuck out. He's really good at that. Even with a bum leg."

Mami turned around and went upstairs. Mary Beth turned and glared at her brother. "This is all your fault."

Johnny scowled. "I couldn't chain him down. He probably didn't want to deal with the police. I don't blame him for that."

Mary Beth looked up to see both her parents coming downstairs. "Sawyer's not here?" her *daed* said.

She nodded. "I came downstairs and he was gone. We have to go find him."

Daed moved to stand in front of her. He held her shoulders. "*Nee*, we don't. This is a matter for the police. If we bring him back here, he'll just leave again."

"But—"

"You know I'm right."

Mary Beth sighed and nodded reluctantly. "It's not fair," she whispered.

"Maybe not, but that's Sawyer's choice." He let her go. "I'll run next door and call the police. Johnny, do the pigs. Mary Beth, help your mother with breakfast. I'm running late as it is, and I have to get ready for work."

Johnny immediately went to care for the pigs while Mary Beth followed her mother into the kitchen. Why had he left? Didn't he trust her parents? Surely he understood that if he could trust her and Johnny, he could trust their whole family.

When their father returned, he met them in the kitchen. Johnny had just returned from the barn. "Any news?"

Daed shook his head. "*Nee*, but they've been out look-ing for him all night. There's nothing else we can do." He looked at both Mary Beth and Johnny. "You did the right thing this time, letting us know right away about Sawyer coming here. I'm proud of you."

"Does this mean we're not grounded?" Johnny asked, hope shading his tone.

Daed looked at him, frowning. "*Nee*. You broke the rules, even though your intentions were *gut*. You should have come to your *mami* and me when you first discovered the *bu*." Then he looked down at Mary Beth. "And you, *dochder*, should have never been at that old barn in the first place."

"But if I hadn't been there, we wouldn't have found out about Sawyer."

"If God had wanted to bring Sawyer into our lives, he would have found a way. A safer way, one that didn't involve disobedience. But we'll talk about your punishment later. Right now it's time to eat so I can get to work."

Later on that morning, Mary Beth finished cleaning the kitchen and watched Micah while her mother started her sewing. Everything was back to normal, or so it seemed. But she knew in her heart that nothing would be the same again. She had changed over the past few weeks. She had learned to appreciate her family and the blessings God had given. She knew what it was like to help a stranger and not expect anything in return. She had also learned that God had a hand in Sawyer's life. Even if Sawyer didn't believe it.

Mary Beth picked up Micah and gave him a kiss on the cheek. "Want to go outside and play?"

"Da!" Micah said, grinning. Mary Beth started to take him outside when she heard her mother call her name from the living room. "Mary Beth! Come here, please."

When she walked into the living room, her mother stood up and met her in the middle, holding a folded piece of paper in her hand. "It's for you. I just saw it a minute ago. It must have dropped off the coffee table." She handed Mary Beth the paper, then reached out for Micah. "Come here, *bu*," she said, taking her son in her arms. "Let's get a drink."

"Da!"

When her mother and brother left, Mary Beth opened the paper. She didn't recognize the handwriting, but she recognized the paper and the drawing of the three kittens drinking milk. She looked at the bottom of the drawing and saw a short note scribbled there.

Dear Mary Beth,

By now you know I'm gone. I appreciate everything you and your family did for me, but I couldn't let the police come and take me away. I can't go back to that foster home. I'd rather live on the run than live with people who don't want or care about me.

At first I thought you and Johnny were just two weird kids that dressed funny, but now I know different. You're both pretty cool, and you have a cool family. I don't know if you realize how lucky you are to have such great parents. I can tell they really care about you.

Maybe someday we'll meet again. I'd like that. But I don't think it will happen. Take care of yourself.

— Sawyer

P.S. I'm sorry I read your journal. I really liked your drawings.

Mary Beth folded the note and ran upstairs. She opened the top drawer of her bureau and put the note inside, then slowly closed the door.

Please, Lord, wherever Sawyer is, be with him.

Sawyer limped along the road, his ankle aching with every step. He'd left the Mullets' a little over an hour ago. He was sure they knew he was gone by now, and he'd half expected them to come after him. But after a while he realized they weren't. He couldn't help but be disappointed. Even the Mullets didn't want anything to do with him, at least the grown-ups. Mr. Mullet probably couldn't wait to call the police on him.

Part of him couldn't accept it, though. If they had been in a hurry to get rid of him, they would have called the police last night, instead of waiting until today. And he had been the one to leave. They hadn't thrown him out.

But he couldn't stick around waiting for the police to come. He could find another truck like he had on his way to Middlefield and jump in the back. Who knew where he would end up? Right now he didn't care.

But . . . if he was honest with himself, he would admit that he did care. He didn't want to leave Middlefield. He liked it here. He liked Mary Beth and Johnny. He even liked their parents, which was amazing, since he barely knew them. And he could picture himself living among the Amish. He wouldn't necessarily want to become Amish, but he wouldn't mind living here.

That wouldn't happen, though. He was on his own.

A car passed by. He didn't even bother to try to flag it down. He needed a truck, like the one he'd snuck into when he left Painesville. It would be tough with his bum ankle, but he would do it. He had to.

He trudged along, so lost in his own thoughts he didn't even notice the car that pulled up behind him. By the time he turned around, it was too late. The police car's lights turned on, and panic overcame him. He tried to run, but his ankle gave out and he fell down, his cheek scraping along the rough asphalt, tearing his skin.

He scrambled to his feet just as the officer reached him. He took a step forward, but the officer grabbed his arm. "You're not going anywhere, son."

Sawyer tried to struggle, but the policeman had him in his grip. Giving up, he slumped, dropped his walking stick, and let the man lead him back to the squad car.

Thirteen

SAWYER LAY on his cot in the group foster home, staring at the yellowed ceiling tiles above him. The room was empty, and that was how he liked it. A week had passed since the police had brought him back, and while his social worker, Mrs. Prescott, had encouraged him to get readjusted, Sawyer had kept to himself. It bothered her that he hadn't settled in with the other foster kids and staff, but so what? It was her fault he'd gone to that terrible family in the first place. He didn't have a choice about anything in his life, especially his social worker. He was stuck with Mrs. Prescott, and she didn't even try to understand where he was coming from.

"Isn't it better here than living on the run, or in some old barn?" she'd said the day after he'd been brought back to the group home by the police.

"No," he'd said, looking straight at her from across the table in the conference room, where she always conducted her meetings. He looked at the closed door, wishing he could knock it down and get out of here. "It's not."

"I don't believe that. I know this isn't a fancy hotel, but at least here you have good meals—"

"The food stinks. Yesterday's special was puke on toast."

"—and a nice bed to sleep on."

"It's a cot. And it smells like wet dog."

"Better than a barn floor." An edge crept into her tone, and her normally unreadable face started to look pinched. She pushed up her black-framed eyeglasses and consulted the folder in front of her, which he guessed was his file. It was probably pretty thick by now, and he bet it wasn't filled with glowing compliments. "The staff tells me you're already putting on weight since you've come back."

"I didn't come back; I was dragged back. Big difference."

"Look, I know you don't like it here, and I promise I'll try my best to find another home for you to go to." She looked over her glasses at him. "But it won't be easy now that you have a history of running away."

He crossed his arms over his chest and glared at her, not saying anything. What would be the point? She wouldn't believe him anyway. He had no doubt his old foster parents had lied to save their own skin, probably to get another foster child so they could keep the money flowing. Those people had everyone fooled.

"Until we can place you in another home, you'll have to stay here. If you're still here when school starts, we'll enroll you in the local school and you'll start classes. If we find you a home after school starts, then you'll be transferred to the district your foster family lives in." She looked up from her paperwork and met his eyes. "Do you understand what I'm telling you?"

"You're telling me I'm screwed."

Her pink lips pulled down into a frown. "Don't get sarcastic with me, Sawyer Thompson. You're lucky you're not in more trouble than you are. Running away is serious. It took time and resources for the police to track you down."

"I heard it took ten minutes."

"It doesn't matter how long it took. What matters is that you don't do it again. If you run away from your next foster family, you might never get placed in another one. Foster parents are very generous, but they don't have unlimited patience."

You have no idea, lady.

"If we can't place you, then you'll have to live in this home until you turn eighteen." She sighed. "I know you've had a hard time the past year. Believe me, I understand."

You don't understand anything.

"And I'm sympathetic. But we have rules, and they're in place to protect you. You could have been hurt a lot worse than just your ankle. You could have gotten sick, or burned up in that fire. Thank your lucky stars you weren't trapped inside that barn." She closed the folder and stood up. "I'll be in touch. Until then try to do what you're supposed to do, okay? Don't annoy the people who are trying to help you. They're just doing their jobs."

That was a week ago, and he had done as she asked and managed not to make waves with anyone. Not because he wanted to, but because it didn't matter one way or another. He doubted he'd be placed in another home. He'd spent enough time here, especially right after his parents died, to know that older kids, especially boys, were hard to place. They had even told him when he went to his last foster home that it might be his last chance. Mrs. Prescott had tried to be positive during their meeting, but deep down he knew it was all an act. He'd be stuck here for the next four years until he turned eighteen. He might as well accept that fact.

Even if he didn't want to.

He rolled over on his side. The rest of the kids were in the rec room playing games and messing around. He didn't want to hang out with them. He wanted to be alone. It was easier that way. But in many ways, it was also harder. He longed for the peace he'd felt in Middlefield, for the quiet of the barn. Being with the Mullets the night after the fire, even when Mr. and Mrs. Mullet were mad at him and Johnny and Mary Beth, there had been a sense of calm that he knew he'd never experience here.

Somehow, after two more hours of tossing and turning, he managed to fall into a troubled sleep.

The month of August came and went, and he started high school, wearing clothes the group home had bought for him. A few kids tried to befriend him, but he wasn't interested. What did it matter, when he might have to move? That would be just his luck. He'd make a good friend, just to lose him in the end. Better to keep his distance. He didn't get hurt that way. And he could deal with the loneliness . . . most of the time.

The third week of school he woke up and got ready to leave for the high school, going through his usual routine and getting in a bit of last-minute studying for his history test later that day. One thing he was determined to do was get good grades. When he got out of this place, he would get a great job and buy a place of his own. Having that goal to work toward helped him get through the day.

Right before eight o'clock he prepared to go outside with the rest of the boys and wait for the school bus to pick them up. He stood to the side of the group and adjusted his book bag over his shoulder. As he did, he saw Mrs. Prescott walking toward him, the heels of her shiny black shoes clicking against the sidewalk.

"There's someone here to see you," she said, looking up at him.

His eyebrows shot up with surprise. "Who?" He couldn't imagine getting a visitor.

"You'll see. Let's go."

"What about school? I have a test today. I can't miss that."

"You'll go later on."

"And what if I say no?" It was the first time since their talk that he'd questioned anything, but her secrecy was annoying. Especially on a test day.

She frowned at him. "You don't want to do that. Now, please, come with me. Right now."

He hesitated for a moment, just to show her she wasn't the boss of him. Then he followed her back into the building. Even though he was irritated, his curiosity was starting to get the best of him.

She led him to a meeting room and they walked inside. He breathed in a combination of stale coffee and carpet cleaner. It made his stomach churn. Then he noticed who was sitting at the table, and his jaw nearly hit the floor.

An Amish couple. At first he thought they were Mr. and Mrs. Mullet, but then he realized they were younger than Mary Beth and Johnny's parents. He didn't have any idea who they were.

"Sawyer, this is Mr. and Mrs. Byler," Mrs. Prescott said. "They're from Middlefield."

He looked at them and nodded but didn't say anything, trying to maintain his cool. He shoved his hands into the pockets of his jeans.

The woman sat perfectly still, her pale blue eyes cast downward and her hands clasped together. The man sat next to her, holding his hat in his hands. They both looked uncomfortable. Sawyer couldn't tell if they were nervous or forced to be here.

"Go ahead and sit down, Sawyer." Mrs. Prescott gestured to the chair across the table from the Bylers.

Sawyer sat down and slouched in the chair. He couldn't imagine what these Amish people were doing here. He wanted to ask if they knew Johnny and Mary Beth, but he wasn't about to show them he cared about anything. Showing weakness was the biggest mistake he could make.

"The Bylers have been going through the fostering process," Mrs. Prescott said with a tight smile. She opened up his file.

"Good for them."

Mrs. Byler looked up at him, her eyes widening a bit. Mr. Byler frowned.

"Sawyer." Mrs. Prescott gave him a warning look and looked at the Bylers. "He's not normally like this. He's a very good boy."

"Except for when I run away. See, I have a little problem with foster parents. I don't like them."

Mrs. Prescott looked like a water balloon about to explode. "Sawyer—"

Mr. Byler lifted up his hand. "It's all right. We know all about him running away." He put his hat on the table. "Daniel Mullet told me."

"You know the Mullets?" The question was out of Sawyer's mouth before he could stop it. He bit the inside of his cheek to keep from speaking again.

"*Ya. Herr* Mullet was the one who told us about you."

"Why would he do that?" Sawyer asked, his curiosity overriding his vow to keep quiet.

"Because he thought we might be interested in fostering you," Mrs. Byler said in a low, soft voice.

Sawyer looked to Mr. Byler, whose expression remained

blank. He didn't look like a harsh man, but he knew from experience that looks could be deceiving. He also wasn't naïve enough to think that just because they were Amish they were anything like the Mullets, even if it was Mr. Mullet's idea.

"The Bylers are interested in fostering you," Mrs. Prescott repeated. "But they wanted to meet you first before they made their decision."

"And we wanted you to get a chance to meet us." Mr. Byler leaned forward, clasping his hands together and resting them on the table. "We thought that would be the fair thing to do."

Sawyer looked at Mr. Byler's hands. They were big, with rough calluses on the sides of the fingers. The knuckles looked cracked and dried.

"I'd like to tell you a little about us," Mr. Byler continued.

"Mr. Byler, that's really not necessary." Mrs. Prescott held up her hand, looking anxious, as if she had someplace she needed to be. Or maybe she just wished she were somewhere else.

Mr. Byler shook his head. "I think it is, Mrs. Prescott. If Sawyer is going to live with us, even for a short time, he needs to know who we are."

Sawyer couldn't believe it. This was the first time he'd met foster parents before being placed in their home. In the past he was dropped off by Mrs. Prescott, told to make the best of it, and left to fend for himself. But these people had come all the way out here to introduce themselves to him. It wasn't a short trip, either. He knew that from experience.

"How did you get here?" he asked.

Mr. Byler frowned. "What do you mean?"

"You didn't drive your buggy, did you? I didn't think your horses could go that far, or very fast."

"They don't," Mrs. Byler said. "We got a ride from one of our Yankee friends."

He couldn't help asking more questions. "Do you live on a farm?"

Mr. Byler shook his head. "*Nee*. But we do have a barn, of course, for our horses and a couple of cows we're raising."

"What about pigs? Chickens?"

"Chickens, *ya*. No pigs. Don't have time for them." He looked confused. "Why do you ask?"

"No reason."

"Do you like animals?" Mrs. Byler asked.

Sawyer shrugged, trying not to look at her. She was younger than his mom had been when she died. Her blue eyes were kind, and each time their gazes met, Sawyer felt a tug inside his heart that he didn't want to deal with.

"We have a few animals," Mr. Byler said. "But I also have my own trade. My father and brothers and I own a carpentry business. We make all kinds of things, from big pieces of furniture to small toys for kids to play with."

Sawyer remembered the wooden train Mary Beth's little brother was playing with the day he had come over and eaten lunch with them. The same day he'd had his introduction to the joys of cleaning the chicken coop.

"Sawyer, you need to be aware that the Bylers don't have any electricity in their house," Mrs. Prescott interjected.

"I know. I've been in an Amish house before, remember?"

Mrs. Prescott pinched her lips together but didn't say anything.

"So then you know we don't have a TV or computer," Mr. Byler said. "We also don't listen to music. We sing during church, but that's all."

"What about school?" he asked. "Where would I go to school?"

"You'd go to the local high school," Mrs. Byler said. "Amish children only attend school until the eighth grade. Since you're already in ninth grade, you'd go to Cardinal High School."

"Would I have to dress Amish?" He'd be laughed out of the school if he had to wear Amish clothes. He wouldn't mind wearing them at the house, but definitely not in public. That wouldn't be cool.

"*Nee*," she said. "You can wear your own clothes. We wouldn't force you to become Amish."

It was starting to sound more and more appealing with every word they spoke. He looked from Mr. Byler to Mrs. Byler. A part of him wanted to leave right then with them, to go back to Middlefield. But a larger part of him was scared. People couldn't be trusted. The only person he could trust was himself, and right now he wasn't even sure of that.

The room started to feel small, oppressive. Suddenly he couldn't breathe. He shot out of his chair and ran out of the room.

"Sawyer!"

He heard Mrs. Prescott's voice but ignored it and kept

running to the common room. He plopped down on the worn, brown couch and leaned over, his head in his hands. Confusion ruled. What was he supposed to do? He wished the Bylers hadn't even come here. He'd had everything planned out before they showed up. Why did his plans never work out?

"Mind if I sit here?"

Sawyer looked up to see Mr. Byler standing by him. He steeled his emotions and looked away. "Don't care."

"Thanks." He sat next to Sawyer and rested his elbows on his knees.

Sawyer leaned back against the couch, staring straight in front of him.

Mr. Byler spoke. "I just wanted you to know that if you don't want to come live with us, that's okay. Anna and I would understand. It's not easy for someone who hasn't grown up Amish to live the way we do. It's hard to adapt. Just know that we're not interested in making you Amish."

"Then why are you even bothering with me?"

"Because Mr. Mullet thought you were worth bothering with. I have to say now that I've met you, I think you are too."

Sawyer couldn't help but look at him. "I don't believe you. You've only known me a couple of minutes."

"*Ya*, but sometimes you can tell a lot about a person when you first meet him."

"Yeah? What can you tell about me?"

"That you're hurting."

"Really? What gave you the clue? Oh yeah, probably my parents getting killed. That's a real bummer." As soon as he spoke, Sawyer wished he could take back the words. This guy didn't deserve his sarcasm. He should reserve that for people who did, like Mrs. Prescott. Mr. Byler was only trying to help, and in the most important way possible: he and his wife wanted to take Sawyer in.

But Sawyer still wasn't ready to trust him. He wondered if he ever would be. "I don't get why you want me," he said. "There are lots of other kids. Younger ones. Nicer ones. Ones that don't run away. Those are the kids people want. Not kids like me."

Mr. Byler sat back against the couch and looked at Sawyer, his expression calm. "I don't know about other people, but my wife and I want you. We believe the Lord has led us here. We can't have children of our own, but God has blessed us in other ways. If we can give a child, any child, a home of his own, we'd like to do that."

Sawyer bit his bottom lip, taking in Mr. Byler's words. Then he asked, "How many kids have you fostered?"

"None. You would be our first."

"So I'm an experiment, then."

He shook his head. "*Nee.* Not at all. Look, here's what Anna and I are offering you. Come stay with us for a month. See how you like living with an Amish family."

"Family? I thought you said you didn't have any kids."

"We don't, but Anna's mother and uncle live with us. Plus I have five brothers and sisters, a nephew, and three nieces. You'll see a lot of them. We're all really close."

"I have an uncle," Sawyer said. "He's in jail right now."

Mr. Byler raised a dark eyebrow. "You don't have any other relatives?"

He shook his head. "A couple. They didn't want me, though."

Sadness entered Mr. Byler's eyes. "I didn't know."

"There's a lot you don't know about me."

"I can say the same thing about me and my family. But I'd like to get the chance to know you. And for you to know us."

Sawyer slumped farther down on the couch, staring straight ahead. "Did you say you know the Mullets?"

"Yes."

"How are Mary Beth and Johnny doing?"

"Fine, as far as I know. I saw them at church last Sunday. They seemed pretty happy. Just like they always are."

So much for them missing him.

Mr. Byler stood up from the couch. "I know this is a lot to consider, and I want you to know that Anna and I won't be offended at all if you decide not to stay with us. Think about it, and let Mrs. Prescott know. We're just a phone call away."

"I thought the Amish didn't have phones."

"Since my family owns a business, we have a business phone. Mrs. Prescott has the number. She just has to call us with your answer, and we'll be out here to pick you up. Not in the buggy, though." He grinned. "You'll have to make do with a car."

Mr. Byler extended his hand to Sawyer. "It's been nice

meeting you. We'll be praying for you as you make your decision. Just remember this—you said that no one wanted you. But Anna and I definitely do."

As Mr. Byler walked out of the room, Sawyer stood up from the couch and started to pace, his eyes burning with unshed tears. Since his parents had died, he'd never had anyone tell him they wanted him. None of the foster parents, or the people who worked in the home, or even Mrs. Prescott. Now here was a guy he'd just met, saying he and his wife wanted to give him a home.

As had happened when his parents died, in a short span of time his whole life was turned upside down. But instead of decisions being taken away from him, he now had one to make. And he had no idea what to do.

Through Mary Beth and Johnny, he knew the Amish to be kind people. Yet there was no guarantee the Bylers would be that way, or that they wouldn't change once he started living with them. And what about the electricity thing? Could he live without that? He'd managed all right when he was on the run, but that was because he'd had no choice. At least here he had TV, although the programming was monitored. Could he live without TV? A phone? A computer? Lights?

He looked around the room, taking in the pale green walls that needed a new coat of paint, the old furniture, the scuffed tile . . . and he weighed his options. Neither of them seemed very good at the moment. If he chose to stay in the group home, he knew what would happen—he would live here and attend school until he graduated, then leave at age eighteen. He would keep his distance from the other boys and focus on finishing school, getting a job, and possibly going to college. Life would be predictable, routine.

And lonely. The people here didn't care about him, not really. They looked after his welfare and made sure he was okay, but when their work shifts were over, they went home to their families. To the people they loved. Like he used to do when his parents were alive.

If he chose to live with the Bylers, there would be more risk, more of the unknown, even though he knew something of the Amish from his time in Middlefield. But as much as he tried to convince himself otherwise, he couldn't help but hope that maybe, possibly, they would come to care about him.

What should he do?

We'll be praying for you as you make your decision.

Sawyer remembered Mr. Byler's parting words. Maybe that's what he needed to do. It certainly couldn't hurt.

Feeling awkward, he knelt down in front of the couch, looking around first to make sure no one was watching him. He folded his hands like he'd seen people do on TV sometimes on Sunday mornings, and started to pray.

I don't know what to say or do, God. I need help, and I'm hoping you can give it to me.

Fourteen

MARY BETH helped Micah out of the buggy and handed him to her mother. It was the middle of September, and they had finally gotten a break from the summer heat. This Sunday morning was cool and pleasant, and as she and her family walked to her friend Katherine Yoder's house for Sunday service, she found herself in a good mood. Those had been few and far between since Sawyer had left.

Her mother had told her that her father had talked to Lukas Byler about taking in Sawyer. And Lukas had said that he would talk it over with his wife, that they would think and pray about it. That was the last she'd heard about it. She'd even tried to listen to some adult conversations to see if she could ferret out some news. Eavesdropping wasn't a good thing, but she didn't know any other way to find out if the Bylers had decided to bring Sawyer back to Middlefield. But if they had, everyone was being tight-lipped about it.

After a couple of weeks of seeing the Bylers at church

without Sawyer, she knew they had decided not to give him a home. She had been so disappointed, and Johnny had too. But she couldn't be mad at them about it. It was their choice, and her father hadn't been too confident that the Bylers would agree to it anyway. Still, that hadn't stopped Mary Beth from keeping Sawyer and the Bylers in her prayers. A few weeks later, while she hadn't forgotten about Sawyer, she knew she had to let go of her hope that he would come back.

Three hours later, after the end of the church service, Mary Beth searched for her friend Katherine and found her cornering Johnny in the backyard. She had him backed against the white wooden fence that surrounded the yard. He looked at Mary Beth with a helpless expression, and she thought he mouthed the words *help me* at her. With a small smile, Mary Beth turned around and walked away. If Johnny didn't want to have anything to do with Katherine, he needed to tell her, for both their sakes. It wasn't fair to string Katherine along. She couldn't get involved in that.

A few of the older kids were setting up a volleyball net, and some of the younger boys had already started a game of baseball in the back corner of the Yoders' yard. Their property was twice the size of Mary Beth's parents', and there was plenty of room to spread out and enjoy the afternoon.

"C'mon, Mary Beth." Another one of her friends, Rachel, waved to her while she was standing by the volleyball net. She moved the ribbons of her *kapp* over her shoulders. "Play with us!"

"Not this time. But *danki* for asking."

Rachel shrugged, then turned and talked with another one of the girls standing nearby.

Mary Beth walked to the far edge of the property, her journal tucked under one arm. She leaned against the white wooden fence and stared out into the empty field behind it. Purple, yellow, and white wildflowers danced among the tall grasses, which swayed in the autumn breeze. Since the barn had burned down, she missed having a place to escape to, especially now that school had started and things were busier than ever at home. She used to resent having to do so much work. Now she was thankful for it, and for her family.

That didn't mean her brothers weren't annoying. Or that she didn't long to be by herself sometimes. Because they were and she definitely did. She knew she'd always need her quiet time, in which she could draw and write and enjoy the peacefulness of being alone.

She touched the rough wood and listened to the commotion behind her. Soon the voices faded away as she focused on the herd of black-and-white Holstein cows in front of her. Some were eating grass, others were standing still except for the swish of their tails, and a couple were lying down. Flipping open her journal, she took her pencil from the coiled binding and started to sketch the scene. She was nearly done when she heard a voice in her ear.

"Hey."

She whirled around, and her eyes widened. "Sawyer?"

He grinned. "Yep. It's me."

He had grown a little taller since she'd last seen him. His hair was cut short over his ears, and he was wearing brand-new Amish clothes. Unable to stop herself, she touched his arm, then drew back. "What are you doing here?"

"Hanging out." He leaned against the fence and stared out at the field. "Checking out the cows." Then he looked at her. "Staying with the Bylers."

She tilted her head. "You're what?"

"I'm staying with the Bylers now. They came and picked me up on Friday." He dropped his head for a moment, then looked back up. "I'm still not sure about this whole pioneer living thing you have going on, but I think I can get used to it. Maybe."

Mary Beth smiled. "Wait until I tell Johnny."

"Already did. I think he was more excited that I gave him an excuse to get away from that girl who was talking to him. He sent me over to come get you to play volleyball. They need one more person."

"Why don't you play?"

"I'm thinking about it. Never played much volleyball back home, though."

"Then I guess that's another thing you need to get used to." Mary Beth closed her journal.

Sawyer's gaze landed on the notebook. "I'm really sorry I read your journal."

"I know. I got your note. And it's okay. I shouldn't have gotten so upset about it."

"Yes, you should have. That was wrong of me. Don't worry, it won't happen again."

She pressed the book against her chest. "Don't worry, I won't let it. I'm not letting this out of my sight."

They both laughed, and he looked out at the field again. "I can't believe I'm here. I really thought I'd spend the rest of my life in that group home."

"I prayed that you wouldn't."

"So did I." He drew in a breath. "I'm still not sure about this God thing, Mary Beth. Not completely. But I've been thinking about what you said, about how God cares for me. I think I'm starting to believe it."

"Hey, Sawyer!"

They both turned around to see Johnny running toward them, a huge grin on his face. "Are you coming or not?"

"That depends." He looked at Mary Beth. "What about it? You gonna play?"

Seeing the expectation on both their faces, she nodded. "Sure. I'll play."

The three of them walked to the volleyball net, Mary Beth in the middle. As they divvied up teams, she heard a dog bark in the distance. Turning around, she saw Roscoe heading toward her.

"Johnny!" she called out, then crouched down as the dog approached. "Roscoe's back."

"Where have you been?" Johnny came up and petted the dog. "We haven't seen you since the fire."

Sawyer grinned and knelt beside Roscoe. The dog's tail thumped against the ground as Sawyer rubbed his neck. "I missed him while I was gone. When I was living in the barn, he seemed to come along just when I needed him."

A few of the other kids came over. Sawyer stood and let them give Roscoe some attention. The dog flopped on his back and showed his belly.

"Anyone know who he belongs to?" a girl asked.

"Nope," one boy said. "Seen him around my yard a couple times, but he never stays very long."

Several of the other kids said the same thing, but no one knew whom the dog belonged to, or even his real name. Like Mary Beth, others had made up names for him—Charley, Preston, Moose, even Bandit.

"Should we try to find him a home?" Mary Beth said.

"I like to think he belongs to all of us." Sawyer knelt down and petted him. "I can see if the Bylers will let me keep him. But I doubt he'll stay in one place."

Everyone agreed with Sawyer. Roscoe was a wanderer, and the dog seemed content with moving from house to house. After petting him a few more times, they went back to start the volleyball game. Roscoe was one mystery they would probably never solve.

"Mary Beth, let's go!"

"I'm coming." As she took her place between Sawyer and her brother, she said a quick prayer. *Thanks, Lord. Thanks for bringing Sawyer back.*